"You're safe now," John said. "I'm so sorry."

"The light went out. I heard someone in the tunnel above me. He was there, John."

John shook his head. "You are one tough cookie."

Olivia dropped her gaze to John's chest. "I was on the verge of a heart attack. I'm not tough."

John put one finger under her chin and lifted her face, looking her straight in the eye. "You were confronted with your worst fear in a house that's been in your nightmares for as long as you can remember, and you were still collected enough to find your way down the tunnel to the exit. You're incredible, Olivia."

He stared at her for a moment, the indecision on his face clear as day, and that's when Olivia realized he was going to kiss her. Her heart leaped into her throat as he lowered his lips to hers, kissing her softly, his lips barely brushing her own. The kiss deepened, and her skin, previously cold from fear, began to tingle and warm with desire.

Suddenly, he broke away and took a step back. "I'm sorry. I didn't mean to…"

If she was a betting woman, she'd bet anything that John was more afraid of that one little kiss than she'd been locked in that tunnel.

JANA DeLEON

THE SECRET OF CYPRIERE BAYOU

™ **Harlequin**®

TORONTO NEW YORK LONDON
AMSTERDAM PARIS SYDNEY HAMBURG
STOCKHOLM ATHENS TOKYO MILAN MADRID
PRAGUE WARSAW BUDAPEST AUCKLAND

To my critique partners, Cari Manderscheid and Cindy Taylor, for your constant cheerleading and support on every new venture I take with my writing career. To my friend Colleen Gleason, who always pushes me to action when I'm on the fence. To my friend Tracey Stanley, who tells everyone who will listen about my books. To my daily chat buddy, Leslie Langtry, for always reminding me that we can't take ourselves too seriously. To my parents, Jimmie and Bobbie Morris, for never doubting I could accomplish anything I set my mind to. To Jimmie, Donna and Katianne Morris, for your continued support in an unpredictable career path. To my agent, Kristin Nelson, for venturing into unknown territory and creating my relationship with Harlequin. To my editor, Allison Lyons, for your patience with me in learning the ropes and your enthusiasm for the work itself. It's always a pleasure to work with people who truly love their product. And to my cousin, Cathy Jane, who no longer has an excuse for not reading one of my books, as this one is short.

ISBN-13: 978-0-373-74586-9

THE SECRET OF CYPRIERE BAYOU

Copyright © 2011 by Jana DeLeon

PLEASE RECYCLE
THIS PRODUCT IS RECYCLABLE

Recycling programs for this product may not exist in your area.

www.eHarlequin.com

Printed in U.S.A.

ABOUT THE AUTHOR

Jana DeLeon grew up among the bayous and small towns of southwest Louisiana. She's never actually found a dead body or seen a ghost, but she's still hoping. Jana started writing in 2001 and focuses on murderous plots set deep in the Louisiana bayous. By day, she writes very boring technical manuals for a software company in Dallas. Visit Jana at her website: www.janadeleon.com.

Books by Jana DeLeon

HARLEQUIN INTRIGUE
1265—THE SECRET OF CYPRIERE BAYOU

CAST OF CHARACTERS

Olivia Markham—She makes her living by renting haunted houses and writing about them, but when she rents laMalediction, she realizes it's the house from her dreams. She's determined to figure out her connection, but someone is just as determined to ensure she doesn't.

John Landry—The New Orleans cop is on the hunt for his missing stepsister, and is desperate to find her before she becomes another statistic. He's posing as a caretaker at laMalediction, his stepsister's last known destination, but he can't conduct an investigation with Olivia Markham looking over his shoulder.

Russ Wheeler—The attorney for the Borque estate should have informed Olivia that he'd hired a new caretaker, but failed to mention it. Given the deterioration of the house and grounds, it looks like one was needed long before now.

Sheriff Blanchard—It was clear to Olivia that the small-town sheriff didn't appreciate her appearance in his town, and especially at laMalediction, but was he a superstitious fool or was he hiding something far more earthly?

Tom Breaux—The café owner gave Olivia directions to laMalediction despite the obvious disapproval of the sheriff, but didn't seem happy to learn that not only had she located the house, she intended to stay.

Aubrey Murphy—The old caretaker supposedly took leave due to a family emergency, but none of his family seems to know what the emergency is or where Aubrey is now.

Chapter One

The sky rolled with a mass of gray clouds, and the air became thick with humidity. Olivia Markham glanced anxiously at the swirling sky as she pulled into Cypriere, Louisiana, all five weather-beaten buildings of it. Peering down each side of the street, she searched for signs of life. It would be the first she'd seen in well over two hours of driving deep into the bayous.

A wooden sign swung under the awning of an old brick building to her left. The painted lettering on the sign had long since faded, but Olivia could barely make out the word "café." Surely someone inside would be able to give her directions. She pulled into an open parking space right in front of the café and hurried inside. Bells on the door jangled as she crossed the threshold and the eight or so patrons stopped what they were doing to stare at her.

She paused for a moment, but when any form of greeting wasn't forthcoming she launched into

her own. "Hello," she said. "Apparently, I'm a little lost. Can anyone give me directions to laMalediction?"

The patrons dropped their gazes back to their tables without saying a word. A middle-aged waitress sloshed coffee on her hand and although the hot liquid must have burned, the waitress froze, looking over at a man sitting at the counter.

A man with salt-and-pepper hair and a gold bar pinned on his shirt identifying him as Sheriff Blanchard turned to face her. "Ain't no one lived at laMalediction for over thirty years. What business you have out there?"

No business of yours. Olivia felt her back tighten with aggravation, in no mood to deal with another round of small-town mentality. "I've leased the house for the winter."

"What in the world would you do that for? Winter's wet and the road's cut off from town half the time. Nothing out there for a young lady to do."

"I'm a writer," Olivia said. "Horror novels, actually, and haunted houses are my specialty."

The sheriff inclined his head toward the plate glass storefront. "You'll be wanting to stay in town until the rain stops. Bayou roads are no

place for somebody unfamiliar with Cypriere, especially during a thunderstorm."

Olivia shook her head, the overwhelming urge to race away from these people overpowering any good sense she might have otherwise had. "I need to get settled before dark. I'll take my chances with the rain."

The sheriff narrowed his eyes at her, but before he could say another word the cook pulled a tablet out from under the counter and began to draw a crude map.

"You take the main road east," the cook said and pointed at a line on the map. "There ain't no street signs to follow, ain't no street either when it comes right down to it. It's more like a dirt path, and you're gonna have to find your way by landmarks. I've drawn them on the map and labeled them."

Olivia gave the cook a grateful smile. "Thank you. I'm sure I'll see you again. I'm not much of a cook, and I eventually tire of sandwiches."

The cook gave her a single nod and turned back to the grill, ignoring the sheriff's disapproving stare. Olivia took one step backward toward the door, feeling that she'd already overstayed her welcome even though she hadn't unpacked a single bag. She gave the frowning sheriff a wave, then turned around and left the café.

She glanced at the map, then backed her car up and headed east. What the heck was going on here? She figured laMalediction's bloody history would prevent the more easily spooked from speaking of it at all, but these people lived within miles of the structure. Surely they knew that it was only a house?

She glanced in her rearview mirror for a final look behind her. The sheriff was standing just outside the café, watching her intently as she drove out of town, but when she took a good look at his expression the annoyance she'd expected to see was nowhere in sight. Even though it was easily eighty degrees outside, she felt a shiver run through her.

The sheriff looked frightened.

"DAMN IT!" Olivia jammed her foot onto the brake as the road she'd been driving on disappeared into a wall of cypress trees. She must have missed a turn somewhere. Glancing up at the rolling black clouds, she bit her lip. That creepy sheriff was going to be right. Chances of her beating the storm to laMalediction were growing slimmer by the minute.

If it was the right way to begin with.

The thought ripped through her mind like one

of those bolts of lightning that was surely on its way. What if the cook had meant to get her stranded in the storm?

Stop it!

Imagining monsters when there were none was great for her stories, but she couldn't afford that kind of fantasizing in real life. She looked at the map once more and decided that she must have missed the twisted cypress trees that marked the last turnoff. Backing up slowly, she scanned the brush and finally located the trees almost hidden by a drape of moss and marsh grass. Mentally chastising herself for her earlier fear, she eased her car into the narrow opening. Only a thin strip of illumination from the fading sunlight passed through to the path.

Ten minutes later the light vanished completely and rain began to pour in giant, blinding sheets. Her visibility reduced to almost nothing; she eased her foot off the accelerator, slowing to a crawl. Seconds later her car dipped into a low spot on the path and came to a stop, the tires spinning in place. She grabbed her cell phone from the passenger seat. No signal.

Hitching a ride wasn't likely given the location, and she wasn't going to drive her car out of the hole it was stuck in. Walking was the only

option. So did she brave a monsoon and try to locate a house hidden away in the bayou, or did she follow the path back to town, which would probably take hours?

Suddenly, lightning struck in front of her car, shaking the entire vehicle with its impact. The aftershocks of the blast echoed around her like flashes from a camera, illuminating an iron gate twenty yards in front of her. She felt her pulse quicken. Surely, the house was close. She kept a change of clothes, toiletries, and her pistol in her backpack. That would do for the night. She grabbed the backpack and a flashlight and stepped out into the storm.

The rain pelted her, stinging her face with its force. She lowered her head and rushed along the path as fast as her vision and the thick bayou mud allowed.

Would this house be the one?

She was holding one hand over her eyes to block the rain, straining to make out the jutting edges of the almost invisible structure in front of her when a burst of lightning struck right over the top of the house, lighting up the structure and the grounds surrounding it. She sucked in a breath so hard it made her chest hurt. Her heart pounded in her throat, blocking out the noise of

the storm around her. She felt her fingernails dig into the palm of her hand as she clenched it.

She'd looked for it for eighteen years. And now, she'd found it.

OLIVIA RAN the remainder of the way to the house, sliding to a stop on a covered porch. Her heart raced as she unlocked the massive front door. She felt inside the door for the light switch, but nothing changed when she pushed it up. Shining her flashlight into the pitch-black house, she saw a huge circular staircase in the center of a two-story entry with marble floors.

She pulled off her mud-caked boots and left them on the porch, then closed and locked the front door behind her. Without electricity, the smartest thing to do was find a bedroom and secure it for the night. In houses of this era the bedrooms were usually upstairs, so she grabbed her backpack and started up the spiral staircase to a long hallway.

The first two rooms were being used for storage, but she hit pay dirt on the third. A huge bedroom, complete with king-size bed and adjoining bath. The bedding was dusty but would do for a night. She closed the bedroom door and turned the giant iron key in the lock on the inside, wishing she had the dead bolts from her

luggage. Not that it mattered. A house this old would have secret passageways for servants, and she needed to locate them. Securing her sleeping quarters was her first task when entering old homes, and her need for security at laMalediction was stronger than any she'd ever had.

She started tapping the walls in the far corner of the room, working her way around and listening for a hollow sound or trying to detect flex in the paneling. After an hour of looking she gave up and slumped into a chair in front of an antique desk. When she got her luggage she'd have the tools necessary to do a thorough job. Right now she needed a hot bath and a good night's sleep.

She grabbed a T-shirt and shorts from her backpack, turned on the water in a huge, clawfoot tub and sighed with relief when it came out hot. She shrugged off her damp clothes and slipped into the steamy bathwater. *This is heaven.* Leaning forward, she placed her head under the faucet and began to rinse her short tresses.

And that's when she heard a creaking sound.

She bolted upright and banged her head on the faucet. "Who's there?" she called out.

Only silence greeted her.

She waited a couple of seconds and was ready to decide it was just the house settling when she felt a gentle current of cold air blow across her bare skin. Shivering, she rose quietly from the tub and reached for a thick towel that hung on the wall. She stepped silently onto the floor, cursing herself for leaving her weapon in her backpack, and crept to the bathroom entry.

Her flashlight was propped on a shelf above the sink and it cast a dim glow around her. Without so much as a breath indicating her presence, she leaned into the doorway and peered into the bedroom.

Empty.

She grabbed the flashlight and shined it into the bedroom for a better look. Still nothing. But as soon as she stepped through the doorway, she felt the remnants of cool air pass across her bare arms and knew it hadn't been her imagination. That draft had come from somewhere in the bedroom, and since both the windows and the door were locked tight only one explanation worked. There was another way into the master suite, and someone had used it.

She turned the flashlight on her backpack to see if anything looked disturbed, and that's when she heard a noise downstairs. Standing stock-still, she listened, hoping to hear the sound

again, but there was only silence. Frustrated, she blew out the breath she'd been holding.

It's an old house. It makes noise.

But what she'd heard wasn't the normal creaking and settling of an old house. It was a whooshing sound. Like someone was moving something big—maybe the exit panel to the hidden passageway attached to her room.

Damned if someone was going to get away with spying on her. She hurried into the bathroom and pulled on her shorts and T-shirt, not even bothering to dry off, then grabbed her nine millimeter out of her backpack and slipped out of the bedroom and into the pitch-black hall. She paused a couple of seconds until her eyes adjusted somewhat to the dark, and then lifting her gun next to her shoulder in a ready position she crept down the padded center of the hallway.

At the end of the hallway, she crouched down and peered between the wrought iron banisters of the staircase. The entry was empty and she squinted into the black, trying to make out movement in the sitting room. Nothing.

Holding her breath, she strained to hear, hoping the sound she'd heard earlier would repeat. One second. Two seconds. Three. There it was again.

Now or never.

She took a deep breath and slowly exhaled, then, staying low, she eased down the stairs and slipped behind a life-size gladiator statue in the entry. She peered into the sitting room, and for a moment it looked as if a piece of the back wall shifted. And that's when she heard it—the shuffle of footsteps on ceramic tile.

An entryway that opened to the kitchen stood on the opposite end of the sitting area. She tightened her grip on her pistol and slipped around the corner and into the sitting room. Staying as close as possible to the wall, she made her way around the room and stopped at the edge of the kitchen entrance to listen again.

For a moment there was nothing, then she heard the footsteps, the sound so faint it barely registered. Her pulse was already racing and she felt her heart beating in her chest when she realized the footsteps were getting closer. She flattened herself against the wall and took aim at the entrance. Then the footsteps stopped.

Her heart beat so loudly she was certain it would give her away. She'd stopped breathing altogether. Did she stay put or confront the intruder? Surely, whoever was sneaking around wasn't expecting a woman with a gun. The element of surprise should be on her side. She

closed her eyes and said a silent prayer. Then before she could change her mind she slipped around the corner and into the kitchen.

And that's when he grabbed her.

HE WAS FAST—faster than she would have believed someone could be and still not make any noise. Before she could even zero in on him, he'd disarmed her and had one hand over her mouth, holding in the scream she tried to let out. She felt her heart in her throat and for the first time in her life wondered if this was how it was all going to end, just like a scene out of one of her books.

Suddenly the lights blinked on and he spun her around to face him, one hand still gripping her shoulder.

"Who the hell are you?" he asked, his amber eyes blazing.

The man was probably mid-thirties, tall and despite the hooded jacket he wore, Olivia could tell he was built for action. Olivia yanked her shoulder out from under his hand and took a step back, glancing at his hand that held her gun. "I'm the person with a key. Who the hell are you?" Olivia shot back, hoping her voice didn't sound as shaky as she felt.

"The caretaker. You're trespassing on private property."

"I'm not trespassing. I leased this house, and if you were really the caretaker, you would know that. Who hired you? Wheeler?"

The man's eyes narrowed at her. "You know Wheeler?"

"Look, I've already told you I have a lease. What I don't have is an answer from you. Now, do I have to call the police?"

He let out a single laugh. "Go ahead and try. The landline in the house hasn't been hooked up in years and cell phone service went out as soon as the storm hit."

"Rest assured, as soon as I can, I'll be calling someone about you." She held out her hand, forcing herself to keep it steady. "I'd like my gun, and I'd like for you to leave." She couldn't even breathe, waiting for him to react. This was it. If he wanted to harm her, he had every advantage.

He studied her for a moment, then placed the gun in her hand. At first it surprised her that he'd returned her weapon without an argument, but then she remembered how he'd disarmed her with complete ease and in a pitch-black room. Her stomach clenched, and she realized that even with the gun in her hand she wasn't the least bit

safe. She waited for him to leave, but he just stared at her as if he was sizing her up.

"You always walk around in the dark, half-dressed and carrying a gun?" he asked.

Damn it. Olivia suddenly realized she was standing in the bright light of the kitchen, soaking wet and wearing only a thin white T-shirt and cotton shorts. She crossed her arms and he smirked. "When I'm supposed to be alone," she said, "and I hear someone downstairs, then yeah, I walk around in the dark, half-dressed and carrying a gun."

"Well, you'll be all alone in about five seconds. I suggest you find someplace to park yourself until morning before you shoot someone." He whirled around and left through a back door, slamming it shut behind him.

Olivia stared after him, her heart still racing. What in the world? The only caretaker the attorney had mentioned was supposed to be eighty years old. There was no way the angry hulk of a man who'd just left was the person the attorney had described. She crossed the kitchen and locked the door behind him, then hurried upstairs.

She locked the bedroom door, pulled the antique desk over in front of it, and set the chair on top of it for good measure. Stepping back

to study her handiwork she bit her lip, then glanced around the room. *Ugly green vase in corner. Perfect.* She grabbed the tall, hideous vase from the corner and stuck it on top of the chair. Granted, with its weight, it didn't exactly add anything to securing the door but at least if someone tried to enter the bedroom that way, she'd hear them coming.

There was no way to easily dry her clothes so she toweled off the worst of the bathwater from her hair and body and slipped into bed, propped upright, gun in hand and every single light in the room blazing.

Chapter Two

John Landry let the kitchen door swing shut with a bang as he stepped out into the storm. What the hell was going on? The attorney had never mentioned someone leasing the house, and even if he'd known someone was taking up residence in the little mansion of horrors, the last person he could have imagined was the petite, mouthy, gun-toting spitfire he'd accosted. What kind of woman leased a derelict of a house, hidden away in a bayou, whose locally given name quite literally translated to "the Curse"?

The last thing he needed right now were complications, and women were always a complication. *This* woman could ruin everything.

The rain poured down and he pulled the hood of his jacket up over his head. He walked the length of the house, shining a flashlight behind the bushes that lined the exterior wall. Nothing. Finally, at the edge of the house, he saw them—a set of footprints in the mud just below a window

in an empty downstairs room. He scanned the window and saw the wood chips at the bottom of the frame and the broken lock inside. Someone had pried it open, but there was no way to tell how recently.

He turned his attention back to the ground and followed the footsteps to the edge of the woods that surrounded the estate, where they disappeared in the brush. Damn it! From his window in the caretaker's cottage he'd seen a light downstairs in the main house maybe fifteen minutes ago. It was small and erratic in movement like a flashlight would be, and since the house was supposed to be empty he'd gone to investigate. Then he'd gotten sidetracked with that crazy woman playing detective. Since she hadn't been carrying a flashlight when he disarmed her, John knew he'd missed his chance to catch the real trespasser.

Assuming the woman was telling the truth about the lease and the key, she had no reason to sneak through the woods and break into the house but someone had a reason. A reason good enough to come out in this storm. The question was, did it have anything to do with his case?

He stepped out of the woods and headed across the courtyard to the caretaker's cottage. The last thing he needed was that woman

hovering around, watching his every move, especially when most of them had nothing to do with repairs. That day he'd searched all the downstairs rooms of the main house and had stopped only because the power went out. He'd planned on starting up again as soon as power was restored, but with that woman lurking inside with a firearm it looked like he'd have to wait. John had no earthly idea why the woman would want to lease a house like laMalediction, but first thing in the morning he was going to find out.

Then he was going to figure out the fastest way to get rid of her.

He gave one final glance at the main house as he entered the cottage. The only light was upstairs, probably in one of the bedrooms. He gave the grounds a final glance, but apparently the trespasser was not interested in trying his luck again tonight. Or he'd gotten what he came for and escaped without a scratch.

John pulled off his dirty boots and left them next to the front door, then grabbed a beer from the refrigerator and slid into a chair at the tiny breakfast table that was serving as his workspace. He picked up a plastic bag and studied the bright pink button inside. The button was new, and had no business being on the floor in the library of the main house. A room that by

the amount of dust collecting on the shelves and tables hadn't been cleaned in a long time, quite possibly years. Unless the old caretaker was a fan of bright pink, someone else, most likely female, had recently been in that room.

Unfortunately, John had no way of knowing if the button belonged to his missing half sister. He'd already questioned his mother, who'd indicated that his sister owned quite a few garments in pink, but then, he guessed a lot of women did.

He slammed the bag back down on the table and took a gulp of beer. He was running out of time. John knew better than most that the longer people remained missing, the less likely they were to be found alive. And that was assuming you found them at all.

Finding Rachel dead wasn't an option. If he didn't bring his younger sister home alive and well, he knew with complete certainty that their mother, who was fighting a seemingly losing battle with cancer, would just give up.

He ran one hand through his wet hair and silently cursed the women in his life. Why couldn't Rachel have focused her master's thesis on something other than ancient southern architecture? At the very least, she could have limited her research trips to only those houses that had been

conveniently converted to bed and breakfasts instead of traipsing off to abandoned mansions in the middle of a swamp. There was far less chance of disappearing in a public place, but this forgotten estate, hidden away from the rest of the world, was just the sort of place to come face to face with trouble.

Of course, now that he'd seen laMalediction he could understand Rachel's fascination with the structure. The few press clippings she'd assembled in a folder marked "Research" had created more questions about the house than answers, and John knew his adventurous and highly inquisitive sister would not have been able to have left the "haunted" house out of her thesis work despite its remote location.

His mother was already in a panic, her health rapidly declining, and it had only been three days since Rachel had disappeared. She'd let him know in no uncertain terms that the only thing she would live for was the safe return of her baby. Like the additional pressure would magically give him answers he didn't have.

And now there was another woman in the mix, and from their brief encounter he'd guess she was just as obstinate and determined as his mother. The caretaker job had been an unexpected miracle, giving him legitimate access

to the estate. Now, that access would be under scrutiny that he couldn't afford.

It hadn't slipped his notice that the trespasser had appeared at the same time as the woman. That gun she carried was no toy, and despite the fact that he'd easily disarmed her, he could tell she'd had some training on how to properly use a weapon. He was fairly certain she wasn't the one who'd jimmied that window, but he had no way of knowing if she'd brought trouble with her.

No matter really.

Her presence in the house was trouble enough. Trouble he didn't need.

OLIVIA AWAKENED THE NEXT MORNING with the sunlight shining directly in her face. Startled, she sat straight up in bed and realized she'd fallen asleep clutching her flashlight and Mace. Her pistol was still within easy reach on the nightstand. Squinting, she covered her eyes with one hand and blinked to adjust to the glare. The rain had stopped sometime in the middle of the night and she must have drifted off to sleep. Apparently her subconscious had decided the likelihood of a second intrusion was slim, or her mind was simply too exhausted to care any longer.

She looked over at the bedroom door. The key, desk, table, chair, and ugly vase were all in place, but that didn't make her feel much better. Someone had come into the room last night when she was in the bath, and she'd bet everything she had that they hadn't used the bedroom door. Blocking the door last night had been a necessary thing to "fool" her frantic mind into some semblance of safety, but here in the stark light of day she knew that safety had been as fictional as the books she wrote.

Outside, an engine fired up and she climbed out of bed to have a look. That "caretaker" was on the front lawn, using a chain saw on a couple of large limbs that had fallen in the driveway. His straight dark hair was just a little too long to be considered tidy and his skin had a beautiful tanned glow, either from the sun or perhaps a Creole heritage. She tried not to admire the way he handled the piece of equipment on a limb the size of a horse, but it was impossible not to when he tackled the tree limb as if he had a personal vendetta against the hunk of wood. *If he's not legitimate, he's pretending awfully well.*

She glanced at her watch and groaned. It wasn't even eight o'clock. She grabbed her cell phone from the nightstand and was pleased to see that service was restored. Scrolling through

her contacts, she located the estate attorney and dialed. It was his personal cell and Olivia hoped she woke the man. It would serve him right after her being scared half-to-death the night before, and being left to dodge a potential chain saw murderer this morning.

"Hello," the attorney mumbled.

"Mr. Wheeler, this is Olivia Markham."

"Yes." The attorney sounded a bit more focused than before. "Ms. Markham, what can I do for you?"

"I'm sorry to call you so early," Olivia lied, "but I've run into a problem here at laMalediction."

"What sort of problem? Are you all right?"

"I'm fine, but I got a bit of a scare last night from a man who says you hired him as a caretaker. He obviously wasn't expecting me, either, and it's lucky I didn't put a bullet in him."

Okay, so there wasn't a chance for her to put a bullet in him or she would have taken it, but Wheeler didn't need to know that.

"I am so sorry, Ms. Markham." The attorney sounded completely flustered. "The old caretaker had a family emergency and had to leave unexpectedly. I've been trying to hire a younger, more capable man for quite a while, and Mr. Landry is the first suitable applicant I've had.

The house needs extensive repairs before it can be sold."

"You never mentioned hiring a new caretaker and you should have. And since Mr. Landry appeared as shocked as me, I can only assume you didn't bother to speak to him, either. Someone could have been seriously injured, Mr. Wheeler."

"I apologize. I meant to call both of you yesterday morning but got so busy I forgot. I tried in the evening and last night, but couldn't reach either of you. I assure you Mr. Landry's credentials are fine."

Olivia looked out the window, watching "Mr. Landry" stack the cut branches to the side of the driveway. "Good. Then you won't mind sending me a copy of his paperwork."

"I'm sorry, but Mr. Landry's paperwork is confidential. Without his consent, I can't really send you his information."

"Fine. Then I'll be by your office tomorrow to cancel the lease."

"Wait! Surely something can be worked out. I don't want you to cancel."

"And I don't want to cancel, but as you know, the house is very remote. I have every right to know exactly who I'm sharing space with. If

you're not willing to provide that information, then I won't feel comfortable staying."

"I understand," the attorney said, but Olivia could tell by his tone that he wasn't the least bit happy with the situation. "I will contact Mr. Landry today and explain the situation. I'm sure he'll give me approval to forward his paperwork to you for your review. If not, then I'll relieve him of his responsibilities and find another person for the position. Will that suffice?"

"For now, but I want that paperwork before the day is over. Email all the documents to me. Does Mr. Landry have a first name?"

"John. As soon as I get to my office, I'll contact Mr. Landry and get his permission to forward the documents. Give me a couple of hours."

"Thank you. I'll be looking for it." She flipped the phone shut and tossed it back on the night-stand. The attorney had annoyed her with his forgetfulness and seeming unwillingness to understand the situation he'd placed her in. Did he really think it was acceptable for her to be shut away in the middle of nowhere with a stranger? If so, he'd obviously lost all common sense.

She stretched, touching the floor with her hands, then rose back up, thinking about her

agenda for the morning. First, she was going to brush her teeth, then she was going to put on her mud-caked boots, stroll outside in her makeshift pajamas, and ask John Landry to show her some ID. Then she was going to convince him to help get her car out of the mud.

Piece of cake.

Ten minutes later she stepped outside and walked to the middle of the huge circular drive. She slowly turned to get a good look at it in the daylight. The bizarre angles of the roof, the two round attic windows positioned on each side of the chimney, the stained glass window that created prisms of light in the entry—all of them exactly as she remembered. She took a deep breath and blew it out slowly, her heart pounding in her chest.

She hadn't been mistaken last night. Her view of the house hadn't lasted more than a second before the flash from the lightning had faded, but that one second had been enough. This was definitely *the* house. She crossed her arms over her chest as a chill swept over her, despite the heat and humidity of the early morning. For as long as she could remember, she'd dreamed of this house. Frightening dreams that she awak-

ened from in a cold sweat, but the only thing she ever remembered was the house.

The house she was certain she had never, *ever* set foot in before last night.

Chapter Three

John heard the front door of the main house close and looked up from his work as the woman walked to the middle of the drive then turned and faced the house. She was wearing the same clothes as last night, but then once he'd realized there was no car in the drive and saw her mud-covered boots next to the front door, he'd gotten a clear picture of what must have happened. She'd probably grabbed the minimum amount of necessities and hiked from wherever her car had gotten stuck. He could only hope that the lack of reliable roadways, utilities, and phone service would send her running straight back to whatever big city she'd matriculated from.

Though he knew less than nothing about ladies' shoes, he recognized her boots as an expensive designer brand that his half sister was drooling over the last time he'd met her in the French Quarter for lunch. Fancy, soft leather. Not even a steel toe. Women who spent eight

hundred dollars on a pair of shoes couldn't possibly find much of interest in a dusty old house in a town with only a café and a gas station serving as the local commerce. At least that's what he was banking on.

He picked up several pieces of the branch he'd been working on and carried them to the pile he'd started at the far end of the circular drive. With every step he took, a curse came to mind. He needed to be in that house, looking for something, anything to help him find his sister. That rotten branch could have waited another fifty years by the looks of the rest of the estate, but here he was slaving over debris blocking a drive that no one had used in years and it was all that woman's fault. He flung the wood onto the pile and spun around. It was time for action. He didn't have time to lose.

She stood at the edge of the circular drive nearest the house, with her back to him. He paused for a moment wondering what in the world she was doing, staring up at the roof of the house, following the lines from one end to another, but then he set his jaw and strode up behind her.

"Not much to look at in the daylight, is it?" he asked, wondering why she still hadn't

turned around when she should have heard his footsteps.

She jumped at the sound of his voice, but her gaze remained focused on the house. "No, I guess it isn't," she said, although she didn't sound convinced. Finally, she turned to face him, a pleasant, but determined look on her face.

Uh oh. He'd seen that look before. His mother and sister wore it very well, especially when they wanted something. Well, he didn't care what Fancy Shoes wanted. He wasn't agreeing to anything.

"I spoke to Mr. Wheeler this morning," she began, "and he assured me he hired a new caretaker. He'll be calling you as soon as he gets into the office to get your permission to forward your employment paperwork to me. If you don't mind, I'd like to see some identification now."

"And if I *do* mind?"

"Then he also assured me that if I was uncomfortable, he would ask you to leave."

John's jaw clenched so hard it ached. She held all the cards. He couldn't afford to lose the job, and he definitely couldn't afford Ross Wheeler digging deeper into his background to placate some crazy woman. The New Orleans police had already asked the attorney for permission to search the estate, but unless they

produced a warrant, Ross Wheeler wasn't going to allow a bunch of law enforcement officials to "tromp through a house of valuable and delicate antiques."

The Cypriere locals claimed they'd never set eyes on his sister when questioned by the New Orleans police, and without any proof whatsoever that Rachel had ever been to laMalediction, there was no chance of getting the warrant Wheeler required. If Wheeler found out John had lied about his real purpose for wanting the job, he'd have every right to press charges against John and the New Orleans police department. And since the department hadn't exactly sanctioned what he was doing, there would be fallout all the way around.

"I assume my license will do," he said as he reached into the back pocket of his jeans and pulled out his wallet. He pulled his license from inside and handed it to her, biting his tongue as she looked at the license, then handed it back to him.

"Thank you, Mr. Landry," she said and tentatively stuck her hand out. "I'm Olivia Markham. I'm sorry we got off on the wrong foot, but a single woman can't be too careful these days."

John started to ignore her hand, but her words resonated through his head. *A single woman*

can't be too careful these days. If only Rachel had paid attention when he said the exact same thing to her. And here he was angry at a woman for doing just what he would have advised. He shook her hand, momentarily surprised at the firmness of her grip.

"I understand," he said. "I would apologize for scaring you last night, but since that's exactly what I was trying to do at the time, I guess it wouldn't exactly make sense. Wheeler should have contacted both of us. Last night could have been ugly."

Olivia looked relieved. "Yes, it could have, and I gave him a big piece of my mind this morning. In fact, I got him out of bed in order to do so, and I have to admit that I got a small amount of satisfaction out of it. I know Mr. Wheeler will be calling you later, but I'd be happy to show you a copy of my lease."

"That won't be necessary, Ms. Markham. You don't exactly fit the profile of a swindler or thief. And since the road to the estate is hardly a highway, I can only assume you actually have business here or you would never have found the place." With any luck, she'd tell him what that business was and he could figure out a way to use it to his advantage.

She waved a hand at the debris on the drive. "I

know you're busy with the mess from the storm, but I really need a favor. My car got stuck last night in the rain, and I'm afraid it's completely blocking the path to the estate. Can you help me get it out?"

John's thoughts swirled around, trying to zero in on the decision that might push her into leaving. He couldn't outright refuse, as then she'd have ammunition for Wheeler to dismiss him but then he also needed to discourage her from staying. "I think there's a mechanic in town with a tow truck. It would probably be better if you called him in case there's also something wrong with the car." Surely Olivia "Fancy Shoes" Markham wouldn't isolate herself at the estate with no way to leave, gun or no.

Olivia frowned. "I hope nothing is wrong. The rental company isn't likely to drive all the way out here to give me a replacement. Look, I know towing my car isn't what you were hired to do, but I couldn't help but notice a truck parked at that little house across the driveway so I thought maybe you could help. I just want to get my clothes and equipment into the house, and then I promise I'll be out of your hair."

John felt himself relenting and silently cursed his mother for training him to assist helpless females. Surely it was meant to be a matter of

manners and not a burden, but it didn't feel that way at the moment. "If that's what you think is best. I think I saw a chain in the storage shed. I'll be back in a minute."

He carried the saw to the storage shed and dug out a chain he'd seen the day before. There was still the glimmer of hope that the car wouldn't run. He could tell by Olivia's expression that she hadn't thought of that possibility until he'd mentioned it. It was also clear she wasn't happy with the thought. Best case, the car would have to be towed back to New Orleans and she'd stay there a few days waiting on a replacement. Those few days might just buy him the time he needed to finish searching the house.

Worst case, the car might make it to the house but stop working afterwards. That was something he was fairly certain he could arrange.

OLIVIA WATCHED John walk away, completely confused by the man. He was abrupt and she got the impression he wanted to be rude most of the conversation but it seemed like something was holding him back from saying what he really wanted to say. Since Olivia was used to dealing with either New Yorkers, who tended to be very direct, or with B&B owners, who tended to be overly accommodating, John Landry was definitely a departure from the norm.

Her thoughts were interrupted by her cell phone ringing. She reached into her shorts' pocket and pulled it out. Speaking of New Yorkers, it was her editor. Great. She wasn't exactly on schedule for this book, and wasn't looking forward to admitting it. "Hello, Irene," she said, trying to sound cheerful.

"I never heard from you yesterday and got worried. Is everything all right?"

"Oh, no. I was supposed to call." Olivia smacked her forehead with her palm. "I am so sorry. I didn't mean to worry you."

"That's okay. It's just unlike you to forget to call, so I figured I'd better check in. So I gather you made it?"

"Sort of. There was a huge storm last night as I was driving in. The house is basically buried back in the bayou with only an overgrown dirt path to get to it. The car got stuck a ways from the house, and I had to make a run for it. There was absolutely no cell phone service. There was no electricity either. In fact, without my luggage there was a whole lot of nothing."

"I don't know why you insisted on that house. It's the worst of the lot as far as convenience, location, communication and just about everything else. Are you sure you want to do this? There's

that lovely house in Boston that's been converted to a very nice B&B. It has a spa…."

Olivia took a second to imagine a hot shower and a mattress less than fifty years old. "Don't tempt me. I know this wasn't the location you wanted, Irene, but I think the story is here. My mind is already whirling with possibilities, and I never got that feeling in the other house."

"I suppose," Irene said, but Olivia could hear the disapproval in her words. "Well, I hope this problem with your car hasn't set you behind. Howard's called twice this morning wanting a status report, and he's frothing at the mouth like a demon child."

Damn. Howard was the vice president, and he disdained his company's recent foray into what he called "mass market trash." The fact that Olivia and the other authors of that "mass market trash" were the only thing keeping the publisher afloat in a tenuous market seemed to make him even angrier. If Howard had his way, the publisher would only print thick coffee table books with bizarre photos of fruit and dead flowers. Or the obscure literary journal that would sell five or six copies, purchased by the author's family to see if they were mentioned.

Olivia bit her lip, then finally blurted out what she needed to say. "If I run into problems

with the car, I might have to backtrack to New Orleans for a day or two. I know I'm already behind my normal schedule for finishing a rough draft because of the time it took to work out the lease arrangements here, but if there is a delay I don't see it being more than two days, max." She clamped her mouth shut, realizing she was rambling.

For a couple of seconds there was dead silence on the other end of the line, and Olivia steeled herself for the disapproval that was surely to come.

"I don't have to remind you that marketing has already spent a literal ton of money on this book," Irene said. "The book that you seem to find excuse after excuse to delay."

"I know this is an important release, and I promise you that I'll make up the time as soon as I've gotten everything under control here."

"Is there something else wrong? You don't sound like yourself, Olivia. You sound like you're on the ragged edge of sanity."

"Everything will be fine. I think I'm getting a little jumpy and starting to panic. I guess I'm overreacting."

"Really? That's interesting considering you're the most organized, controlled person I know, and that's saying a lot. What's got you spooked?

The storm? I know it can't be the house itself. It's not like you haven't done this a time or two before."

Olivia looked up at the house and shook her head. "I don't know, exactly. I mean, this is definitely the most remote location I've ever been to, and the house hasn't been occupied in over thirty years, so that gives it a much different 'feel' than the others. And given that I arrived in the midst of a monsoon, and had no power… then there was a run-in with the caretaker."

"What run-in?"

Olivia described the scene in the kitchen from the night before. "I called the estate attorney first thing this morning and everything checked out," she finished, "but it scared the life out of me."

"I should say so. Well, if you won't consider a more civilized location for this book, will you at least consider relocating to a hotel in New Orleans until I can arrange you security of some sort? I can't afford for some angry caretaker to distract you from your work. There's a firm in New Orleans that I've used before. I could probably get someone assigned to you within a week. You could work from photos until then."

"A week at a hotel in New Orleans. I have to admit, it's very tempting, but I really think the

story is here. I'll call you back if I change my mind."

"Okay," Irene said, but didn't sound convinced. "Promise me if you run into any problems that will delay this book, you will let me know immediately. Olivia?"

Olivia looked over at the storage shed as John walked out carrying a long length of chain, the grim look on his face clear as day, even from a distance. She was apparently three for three in making people's day this morning. "I promise. Look, I've got to go. I'll let you know in a couple of hours what I'm going to do."

She flipped her phone closed and dropped it back in her pocket. If Olivia was a betting woman, she'd bet everything she had that she was the source of John Landry's discontent. But if she was such a trial, why bother with her at all? He certainly could have made up any sort of excuse for not wanting to tow her car with his truck.

Granted, she could cost him his job if she wanted to be a real bitch about it, but was a handyman job in the middle of nowhere all that great a gig? With all the hurricane reconstruction going on in New Orleans, the last place she'd expect to find a young, able-bodied man would be hidden away in Cypriere.

In fact, the more she thought about it, the more John Landry didn't add up at all.

THE MAN WATCHED HER from his hiding place behind the overgrown bushes that surrounded one piece of the drive. While he would have recognized Olivia Markham from her photo in the back cover of her books, the picture really didn't do her justice at all. She had that fine facial bone structure that seemed to grace only a few each generation, and a toned but curvy build. The entire package was reminiscent of the old portraits of upper class women, which was appropriate if one considered the circumstances.

Her conversation with the caretaker concerned him some. It was obvious that the caretaker wished Olivia would leave, but given everything he knew about things to come, that just didn't make sense. Thirty years he'd been waiting for things to fall into place, for things to align as they were supposed to when the time was near. Surely, the caretaker wouldn't have come unless he had a part to play.

The person Olivia had talked to on the phone concerned him more. For whatever reason, he'd gathered from their conversation that the person Olivia had been speaking to had suggested she leave the house and go to New Orleans for a

week. And it had sounded like Olivia was considering it. No matter what, he had to make sure that didn't happen. He'd been watching the moon, and was certain—the day and hour for fulfilling the prophecy was fast approaching.

The first woman who'd come to the house hadn't given him the answers he was looking for. He'd thought she was the one. She had eyes like the photo, but maybe he had been wrong. Olivia didn't have eyes like the photo, but otherwise, the resemblance was clear. Surely, Olivia was the one. It had been decades since a woman had even set foot at laMalediction. Now, there had been two in one week. One of them had to be *the* one.

Regardless, neither of them was leaving laMalediction until the prophecy was fulfilled.

Chapter Four

John glanced in his rearview mirror at Olivia's car. Despite being stuck in a good foot of mud, it had started right up and was managing the drive to laMalediction. It figured. He'd hoped an out-of-commission vehicle would send her running to the city for a replacement, at least for a couple of days, but no such luck. Now he needed a plan to work around Olivia Markham without her alerting the attorney that something was suspicious.

He parked in front of the mansion and waited until Olivia pulled up beside him. She was smiling when she got out of the car. "I'm so relieved it's running," she said and reached back into the car to pop the trunk.

John couldn't have disagreed more, so he just nodded and looked over at the boxes in her trunk. Whatever Olivia Markham was doing at laMalediction, it looked like she'd packed enough for a long stay. "There's no food or supplies at the

main house. I picked up bread and lunch meat for myself, but I wasn't expecting company."

Olivia waved one hand at the boxes. "I brought supplies," she said. "Just some bagels, peanut butter, chips and drinking water. I've gotten in the habit of traveling with a minimal amount of food. I figure in another day or two, I should be able to drive back into town, right?"

"Probably." He held in a sigh. Apparently, it was going to take more than bad weather, a reported haunted house, flaky electricity, no cell phone connection and a lack of groceries to get rid of her.

"Do you need some help moving that stuff inside?" Maybe he could figure out why she was here and that would give him an angle.

"Seriously? That would be great." Olivia pulled the first box out and shifted it to balance. "The boxes are all electronics, so please be careful."

Electronics? John grabbed a large box from the trunk and followed her into the house. Seemed a strange hobby at a house that lost power every time it rained.

Olivia stopped in the entryway. "I don't suppose you know of a library or study in the house? A place with a good desk or table for working?"

John nodded. The library was where he'd found the pink button. "There's a library straight back past the stairwell, then turn left down the hall."

"Great." Olivia headed toward the hallway. "I didn't know if you'd taken stock of the house yet or were only concentrating on the outside maintenance."

John followed behind her, his mind forming an idea that just might get him around Olivia until he could get rid of her. "Actually, I'm supposed to be working on the main house, but I didn't want to disturb you this morning, so I worked in the drive. I'm an early riser."

Olivia stepped into the library and placed her box on a long, dusty table in the center of a room with floor to ceiling bookcases on every wall. "I love this," she said, looking around the room. "All it needs is a good cleaning."

John placed his box on the table. "I'm not going to disturb your work if I go about my business upstairs, am I?"

"I doubt it. What are you doing, exactly?"

"Right now," he said, as he formulated the lie, "I'm just assessing everything and making a list of necessary repairs so that Wheeler can order the supplies I need. I do a lot of banging wood and moving stuff, though."

Olivia waved a hand in dismissal. "I've trained myself to write in almost any circumstance. I acclimate to the sounds of a new house quickly, so your work shouldn't bother me at all."

John stared at her for a moment, not certain what to say. A writer? He would have understood if she was an antique dealer looking to catalogue the furniture or a real estate agent looking to get a contract on the house, but why in the world would someone choose laMalediction as a place to write a book? "You're writing a book?"

Olivia nodded. "I know. Most people find it strange, but this is my niche. I stay in a reputed haunted house and write a ghost story about it. My next book is due soon and it will be set at laMalediction."

"Haunted houses? Do you believe in that sort of thing?"

Olivia pursed her lips. "I think a fair statement would be that I don't limit the universe to what I understand. I've seen things I can't explain, but that doesn't mean there isn't an explanation." She smiled. "The good news is I don't spook easily, so you won't have to worry about catering to a damsel in distress."

John nodded, feeling his options lessening by the second. "I'll go grab another box," he said and left the library.

I don't spook easily.
She said that like it was a good thing.

OLIVIA DROPPED the filthy sponge in a bucket of dirty water. Three hours of scrubbing and the room was finally fit for habitation. She sank down on the floor and leaned back against one of the now-sparkling maple bookcases. It really was a beautiful room. In fact, everything she'd seen of the house so far was gorgeous. It was a shame that no one lived there enjoying it, although she guessed most people wouldn't enjoy being sequestered out in the bayou with only a small town of strange people and a swamp of all kinds of creatures as company.

A crash above her caused her to jump and she slowly pulled herself up from the floor. John Landry had been making good on his noise-making promise. He'd been banging and knocking upstairs as long as she'd been cleaning downstairs. She sometimes wondered if he was creating more work.

She grabbed the bucket, headed to the kitchen, and dumped the dirty water in the sink. She rinsed the bucket and placed it upside down in the sink to dry, then pulled a bottle of water from the refrigerator and rubbed it across her forehead before taking a huge swig of it. The humidity

was something she'd expected to encounter but it was worse than what she'd imagined, especially with no air conditioning.

She grabbed a bag of potato chips from the kitchen counter and headed back to the library. Unpacking and setting up her laptop and printer was next on her list, then she'd be ready to work. No more excuses. She smiled when she thought about all the ideas that were already flowing through her mind for the book, and then stopped short when she stepped into the library.

Something is wrong.

She scanned the empty room. Nothing seemed out of place, but yet, she knew it wasn't like she'd left it. All five of her boxes were still stacked at one end of the long table and at the other end of the table was a lamp. She felt her breath catch in her throat. A lamp that used to sit on a tiny table on the far wall.

Taking a step closer to the table, she checked her boxes more closely. They were still sealed and didn't appear to have been shuffled around at all. A loud thump upstairs caused her to jump. Her water bottle slipped out of her hands and onto the floor.

Get a grip. It's just John, you know, the man you told you didn't spook easily.

Could John have moved the lamp just to

mess with her? She thought about her trip to the kitchen, trying to recall if she could still hear him banging around when she'd been cleaning the bucket but she'd grown so used to the noise that she simply didn't know. Surely, that was it. He was playing a joke on her. Trying to prove she wasn't as tough as she thought she was. She crossed her arms across her chest, suddenly chilly in the previously stifling room.

Well, it wasn't a very funny joke, and she wasn't going to stand for it.

She picked up her water and set it on the table with a thump, then strode down the hall and up the stairwell, ready for battle. She found John in a bedroom at the back of the house, probably positioned over the library downstairs, and he was covered all over with something white.

One glance at the gaping hole in the ceiling and the mess surrounding him on the floor gave her a clear idea of where the white substance came from. "What happened?" she asked.

He was standing on a stepladder with his head poked up in the hole in the ceiling. Leaning down a bit, he looked out at her. "Ceiling fell in is what happened. Didn't you hear all that noise earlier?"

She remembered the loud crash she'd heard

when she'd just finished cleaning. "That was the ceiling? Wow. I guess you were standing under it."

"Unfortunately. I thought the light fixture was loose but it was the entire ceiling that was sagging. I barely touched it and the whole thing came crashing down on me." He stepped down the ladder and retrieved a water bottle from the dresser, leaving white tracks everywhere he stepped.

Olivia stared at the white shoe prints then back into the hall. It was dusty and dirty, but not a single white ring in sight.

"Did you need something?" he asked.

"No. I just thought I ought to check and make sure everything was okay...you know, with the noise."

John narrowed his eyes at her. "So you thought I might be injured but waited a good five minutes to come up and check?"

"Yeah," Olivia said as she backed out of the room. "Sorry, you're right. I should have checked sooner, but I was pouring out a bucket of dirty water." She pointed down at his feet. "You might want to take your shoes off before you walk around much more. Not that the place is clean or anything."

John glanced down at his feet and frowned.

"You're right. No sense making it worse." He looked back up at the ceiling and sighed. "This is going to be a real mess to fix."

"Well, I'll leave you to it," Olivia said and fled down the hall.

She checked the front door, but the dead bolt was still securely in place. A quick check of the back door in the kitchen revealed the same thing. He could have taken his boots off before coming downstairs. That would make perfectly good sense, especially if he didn't want her to hear his footsteps on the marble flooring in the entry. But Olivia would swear by his expression that he hadn't even noticed the state of his boots until she'd pointed it out.

Unless he was a very good actor.

Olivia hurried back to the library, determined to hook up her computer, contact Wheeler and make sure she had all the information she could get on John Landry. She stopped short in the doorway.

The lamp was back in place.

JOHN WATCHED Olivia flee the room and shook his head. For someone who claimed she didn't spook easily, the woman looked like she'd seen a ghost. She'd obviously come upstairs for a reason, but whatever that reason was, she'd

changed her mind about it. He didn't believe for one minute it was the crash that had brought her scurrying up the stairs. If she had been that worried about it, a bucket of dirty water would have been the last thing to detain her.

He'd thought about pushing the issue, but finally decided that if something was bothering Olivia, that would likely only work in his favor. Staring back up at the ceiling, he sighed. He'd had no intention of creating more work for whoever replaced him, but that's exactly what he'd managed to do. He dug through the pile of Sheetrock and pulled out the light fixture that had attracted his attention in the first place.

It was coated with Sheetrock dust and any chance of gaining a fingerprint was probably long gone, but he wanted to make sure he hadn't been imagining things. He wiped the dust off the light fixture's ceiling plate with the bottom of his shirt. Just as he'd thought—scratches lined the bottom of the ceiling plate close to the screws that held the fixture in the ceiling.

There was no way to tell if the scratches were new, but John would bet everything they were. The ceiling plate had been wiped clean. That's what had drawn his attention to the fixture in the first place—a shiny plate in a room of otherwise dusty items. He'd brought in the ladder hoping

to get a closer look, but when he'd placed a hand on the ceiling to steady himself, the whole thing had come crashing down.

He looked at the light fixture. Maybe the old caretaker had been aware of the ceiling problem and started taking the fixture down to make the repair. He placed the light fixture on the floor and blew out a breath. He was wasting time. It didn't matter what the old caretaker had intended, or if every upstairs ceiling dropped down on him.

He had to find his sister.

Despite Olivia staying out of his way, this afternoon had been a total waste. He'd found nothing new. No indication that his sister had been on the second floor. And maybe she hadn't been. If she'd even made it to laMalediction, maybe she'd run into trouble before she'd ever gotten the chance to do much poking around.

He ran one hand through his hair, scattering Sheetrock dust around him. What if he'd made a mistake about her destination? What if she'd scheduled her visit to laMalediction on her calendar and changed her mind? If his sister had never been to this house, he was losing valuable time here. If only he could find evidence, anything that told him for certain that she'd been here. The pink button was a sketchy clue, at best.

He pulled his cell phone from his pocket. No messages, but at least it had decent signal strength. He pressed the number for the New Orleans police department and asked for the captain.

"Landry?" Captain Reeves answered the phone. "Where the hell are you? Harrison's been by your apartment twice and says your phone's turned off."

"I went to visit an aunt my mom used to check on. She lives out a ways in the bayou. Cell phone signal's sketchy."

"An aunt, huh? So your sister's missing and your mom's in the hospital, and you want me to buy that you took vacation time to visit some old lady?"

"Yes, sir," John replied, keeping his voice steady. If the captain found out he was at laMalediction after Wheeler had forbidden the police to enter the property, he'd have John's badge. "Is there any news?"

The captain was silent for a moment and John was afraid the man was going to call him on his lie. The captain was no one's fool and knew John about as well as anyone did. Well enough to know that John wouldn't bail on the investigation without a really good reason—like a lead that the police didn't have the authority to pursue.

"Not much. Harrison was just here and said they found a store clerk about twenty miles outside of New Orleans on I-10 who remembers your sister filling up there five days ago."

John felt his pulse quicken. He'd driven past that filling station on the way to laMalediction. Rachel could have been pursuing another house in the same direction, but there was no mention of another house on her calendar until weeks later. At least it was something. "Is the filling station guy certain it was Rachel?"

"Yeah. I got the impression he liked what he saw. Described her and her car pretty well and seemed certain when Harrison showed him the picture."

"But no indication of where she was going?"

The captain hesitated. "He says she asked about Cypriere."

"Damn! I knew it. Now, are you going to get a warrant?"

"I hung up with the district attorney right before you called. It's thin, probably not enough for a warrant, but he's going to ask one of the judges for a favor given this is a cop's family. The judge has a cousin who went missing twenty years ago and was never found. The D.A. thinks he'll be sympathetic."

"How soon can we get access?" If he didn't

have to hide, he could flood the house and grounds with men and equipment. No sneaking around and making excuses. No more hiding behind a stepladder or a chain saw.

"The judge he thinks will give the warrant is out of town for two days."

"You've got to be kidding me! Tell him to get another judge."

"There isn't another judge who's willing to put his neck out. The D.A.'s already asked around on this and been told no. There's entirely too many things that could have happened to Rachel between that filling station and wherever she was headed. Unless someone can put her in Cypriere, then none of the other judges are willing to risk it."

"I don't have to tell you how much time has passed."

"No, you don't. I don't like it any more than you do, but I have to tell you John that if you do anything to risk this investigation, it will not be good for your career. Do not go near that property until we have a warrant. Are we clear?"

"Crystal."

"I mean it, Landry. Do not set foot in Cypriere."

"No problem." John closed the phone. He hadn't really lied. He had no intention of setting foot in Cypriere, the town. If his sister was

going to be found, he had a feeling it would be at laMalediction.

He tucked the phone into his pocket and headed downstairs. There had been no sign of Rachel on the second floor, so he'd save the attic until last. The basement was his next destination and he'd seen an access door in the kitchen. He hurried into the kitchen and almost collided with Olivia.

A camera slipped in her hands, and she clutched it to keep from dropping it. He grabbed her shoulders to steady both of them. "Sorry. I keep forgetting there's someone else here." He looked down at the camera and blinked. "Nice camera."

Olivia frowned. "Yeah, it is. I found it in the cabinet when I was putting up my supplies. I thought maybe it was yours. I was coming to ask."

John's pulse began to race. He'd bought that exact model for his sister for Christmas. "No, but maybe the old caretaker kept it here to take pictures for Wheeler."

Olivia shrugged and handed him the camera. "Maybe so. Guess you'll need it then. I'd start with that ceiling upstairs if I were you. It didn't come down by itself. If there's a leak somewhere it can get way worse for you."

John took the camera and turned it on, pleased that the batteries were good. "You're absolutely right. I think I'll do that now." He left the kitchen, studying the display on the camera. Twenty-two pictures stored.

Maybe one of them would give him a clue to finding Rachel.

Chapter Five

Olivia trudged up the stairs, holding a printout on John Landry that she'd received from Wheeler. She planned to read it again while soaking in a hot bath, but her initial review had shown nothing even remotely questionable. It had taken her an hour to set up her equipment and another hour to finally acquire a decent enough satellite connection to download the documents, but at least that part of the necessary work was done. With any luck, the bath would revive her and she might get a second wind and do a little work that night.

She entered the bedroom and went to retrieve her change of clothes from her suitcase on the bed and that's when she saw it—a small, framed, black-and-white photo lying on top of her luggage. She whirled around and looked into the bathroom, then checked in the hall but saw nothing. Maybe John had left it there when he was doing his repair inspection. Maybe he'd

moved it so it wouldn't be damaged and forgot to replace it.

Except for the fact that there had not been a single photo in the room the night before, it was a perfectly logical theory. She started to set the photo on the nightstand to deal with it later, but then took a good look at the picture. It was a woman in a fancy dress, and had to have been taken a long, long time ago, sometime well before the turn of the century. But the preserved nature of the photo was not what made her gasp.

The woman looked just like her.

Olivia clutched the photo and sucked in a breath, both frightened and excited at the same time. She'd come here looking for answers. Maybe she was finally going to get them. She felt her stomach roll. Who was helping her? That picture hadn't appeared out of nowhere, and it was no coincidence that it had been left in her room.

John was the logical choice. He'd been upstairs working all day. Maybe he'd seen the photo and thought she would find the rescmblance interesting. That must be it. A completely logical explanation, for a change.

Maybe.

But then, if they were the only people in the

house, who had moved the lamp or, for that matter, entered her bedroom the night before while she was bathing.

She stepped into the hallway and called out. "John. Are you still working up here?" No answer was forthcoming, nor could she make out any noise at all. In fact, now that she thought about it she realized she hadn't heard a peep since he'd accosted her in the kitchen and left with the camera.

She slipped the papers on John into a drawer in the nightstand, grabbed the photo and headed back down to the library. While dusting, she'd noticed several photo albums on the bookcases. If they were labeled, she might be able to identify the woman in the photo. She grabbed several of the heavy albums off the bookcases and laid them on the table.

The first one contained color photos and was clearly far too recent. The second book was close to the right era, but the woman was not in any of the photos. In the third book, she hit pay dirt. An eight by ten photo of a woman and a man standing in front of laMalediction. The woman was wearing a different dress, but there was no mistaking the facial features and the hair. This was the woman from the photo.

Franklin and Marilyn Borque, 1861.

Olivia felt a chill pass over her. No, it couldn't possibly be.

"Must be interesting." John's voice sounded behind her and she jumped.

"Oh my God," Olivia said, her heart racing. "I didn't even hear you come in."

He raised his eyebrows. "I wasn't exactly sneaking."

"No, I'm not saying that. I guess it *was* interesting." She looked up at the man, standing in the doorway and bit her lip. Did she come out and ask him if he was messing with her or keep her cards hidden? What if he said it wasn't him? Would she know if he was lying? So far, John Landry seemed a bit of an enigma.

"Look at this," she said and lifted up the photo album before she could change her mind.

John looked at the photo, then her, then back at the photo. "Wow. No wonder you didn't hear me. You look just like her."

Olivia blew out a breath she didn't even realize she'd been holding. "So you see it, too?"

"Hard to miss. Just a little different in the eyes, but really close. Is she a relative?"

Olivia shook her head. "Not that I'm aware of, but then I don't know anything about my family."

John frowned. "But you just happened to lease

this house, and just happened to find a picture that looks like you in the library?"

"Actually, that's something I wanted to ask you about." She picked the smaller photo up off the table and handed it to John. "That picture was on my bed when I went upstairs earlier."

John's head snapped up from the photo and his eyes narrowed on her. "How did it get there?"

"I thought maybe you could tell me."

John stared at her in surprise. "Me?"

"Well, you were upstairs all day. I thought maybe you saw the resemblance and left the photo for me, but I guess not."

John shook his head. "I've never seen this before now, and I've been through every room in this house on the first and second floor."

Olivia studied his expression as he looked back down at the photo then again at Olivia, but he appeared as confused as she was.

"So how did it get there?" she asked.

"I don't know, but I don't like it, and I don't believe it's a coincidence that the photo looks like you. It's easy to fake photos these days, but then the real question would be, who's trying to scare you?"

"No one."

John raised one eyebrow.

"I swear." Olivia raised one hand as if taking

an oath. "I don't have a problem with anyone, and very few people even knew I was coming here. Besides, there's a whole photo album here with the same woman. Do you think someone faked all of it?"

John frowned. "Look, I know you write books about monsters and stuff, but I don't believe in any of that. What I *do* know is that a ghost didn't put that picture on your bed."

"I know. I don't believe it was a ghost, either."

"No one would go to such lengths unless it was personal. Are you sure you haven't hacked anyone off lately? An angry reader, maybe?"

Olivia shook her head. "I don't see how. I don't write under my real name and my publisher is very careful about keeping my real identity a secret."

"I don't suppose your publisher would stoop to scaring you for a better novel, would they?"

"Heavens, no. Something like this makes it harder to concentrate on writing, not easier."

"Well, despite the veil of secrecy you claim you're under, anyone can be gotten to if a person wants to bad enough." He paused for a moment. "I don't think you ought to stay here. Maybe you should go to New Orleans for a couple of days.

Give me a chance to poke around and see what I can find."

Olivia knew that what John said made sense, but she just couldn't bring herself to agree. Olivia didn't believe for a minute the photo was a fake. No one would go to the trouble of creating an entire album just to scare her. Even her editor didn't know about her past. How could anyone else?

This might be her last chance to learn something about her family, to figure out why she kept dreaming about the house. If she left now, she might not have the opportunity again. Whoever had left her the picture was probably trying to scare her, but it had done just the opposite—it had made her determined to stay and check into its authenticity.

"No," she said finally. "I don't respond to scare tactics."

"Olivia, I can't guarantee your safety. The doors to the house have been locked, and if someone was strolling around upstairs, one of us should have heard or seen them."

"Why didn't you see them?" Olivia shot back. "You were working upstairs."

"Not late this afternoon. I finished upstairs and moved down to the basement. If someone

came in through a window or even the front door, I wouldn't have heard them."

Olivia blew out a breath. "Then I suggest both of us start poking around. I don't like the idea that someone besides the two of us has access to this house. They have to be getting in somehow and the dead bolts are in place on both doors."

John hesitated for a second and Olivia could tell he clearly wanted her out of the way, not in the middle, but running didn't fit into her agenda.

"Fine," he said finally. "Where do you want to start?"

"Outside? I mean, that's logical, right? He didn't drop in from the sky."

"He certainly didn't park in the drive and stroll inside," John agreed. "We can walk the perimeter of the house. The ground's soft from the rain. There ought to be footprints." He gave Olivia a nod and headed for the front door. Olivia pulled on her tennis shoes and followed him outside.

THIRTY MINUTES LATER, Olivia tugged off her muddy tennis shoes and set them on the front porch. They'd circled the house twice, searching every square inch of the ground within twenty feet of the house but they'd found nothing. On

the second pass, John never spoke a single word as they searched the grounds around the house, frowning the entire time.

He pulled off his dirty shoes and tossed them next to hers, but he stared across the courtyard, his brow furrowed in concentration. "What are you thinking?" Olivia asked.

He didn't answer her immediately, and after several seconds passed, Olivia wondered whether he was going to answer her at all. Suddenly he turned to face her, his eyes locking onto hers. "You're certain the picture wasn't there before."

"Absolutely." Olivia frowned, wondering where he was going with his line of questioning, then suddenly it hit her and she sucked in a breath. "He was already in the house. That's what you're not saying. That he's been in the house all this time…Oh my God. If there're no footprints then he hasn't left either."

"Maybe not. He could have left out the front door when we were around back."

"But he may still be in there."

"Yeah."

Olivia took a deep breath and blew it out. "Then I guess we better get to looking."

"And start where? There's probably a million places to hide."

"My room."

John frowned. "Why there?"

"Because that first night during the storm someone came into the room while I was bathing." She explained the draft and her theory of secret passageways.

"And then you came downstairs dripping wet, half dressed and toting a gun. Makes a lot more sense now." He shook his head and gave her a begrudging look of admiration. "You've got backbone. I'll give you that."

"I told you—I don't spook easily. And I don't like people messing with me."

John nodded. "I'll bet you're right about a secret passageway. Let me grab my tools from the basement, and we'll start now. I don't want you sleeping in there if we can't secure the room."

Olivia watched as he walked away, wondering about the enigma that was John Landry. He was the stereotypical strong, silent type, but then things got muddy. She could tell he preferred to be left alone, but yet if he felt her security was threatened he jumped immediately into action. Olivia had no doubt that if called for, he'd fight with deadly force. He had a dangerous edge to him, something just beneath the surface that told

her this man wouldn't necessarily play by the rules if it didn't make sense.

I can't guarantee your safety.

John's words flashed through her mind. She knew what he said was true. If someone wanted to get to her they eventually would, but for whatever reason she felt better about her chances here with John than anywhere else without him.

JOHN TAPPED ON A WALL in Olivia's bedroom and listened for a hollow sound, an indication that there was space behind the wall. Olivia's story troubled him on many different levels. He still thought she was hiding something, but he believed her when she said she had no idea who could be behind the intrusions. It was clear to John that someone was playing a game with her, but why? And even though he thought she was still keeping secrets, John didn't think Olivia had an answer to that question, either.

Her proclamation of secret passageways for servant usage was both surprising and frustrating. It was something he hadn't taken into consideration, but would explain why someone had been able to move through the mansion without being seen. Whoever was playing tricks with the photographs knew the mansion intimately, and that led to a whole other set of questions.

Was the intruder someone from Cypriere, or was Olivia's identity not as hidden as she thought it was?

"You find anything?" Olivia's voice sounded behind him.

He rose from the floor to face her and shook his head. "No. All the walls appear solid. What about you?"

Olivia shook her head and gave the room a quick glance. "I didn't imagine that breeze, and there's no other source that could have created it. The windows are sealed remarkably tight given the state the house is in and there's no gap in the door, either."

"I agree."

She gave him a half smile. "With what part?"

"All of it. I don't think you imagined anything, and I think the most logical explanation is that someone entered the room."

Olivia blew out a breath. "I was afraid you'd think I was crazy."

"I never said I didn't think you were crazy. The way you go about making a living is definitely borderline crazy."

Olivia laughed and John smiled back before he even realized it. Despite being in the way, Olivia Markham was a hard woman not to

like. She was tough, logical, independent and definitely not hard on the eyes, especially for a man who preferred an athletic frame and natural good looks to women made up so perfectly they looked as if they'd been varnished.

And she still needs you.

The thought tipped through his mind like a knife and he clenched his jaw. He had no argument for the truth. Despite Olivia's capabilities, she still had a situation on her hands that she couldn't handle alone, which meant that now he had three women who needed something from him. And that was something he'd been trying to avoid.

A bolt of lightning flashed outside the bedroom window and the thunder that followed made the old glass panes shake. "Wow," Olivia said. "Looks like we're in for another doozy."

Her words jolted him from his thoughts and he nodded, willing his mind to return to the business at hand—finding the secret passageway. "Weather report says it should be a short storm, but powerful."

"You zoned out there for a minute," Olivia said. "Is anything wrong?"

"No. Just thinking." He pointed to the wardrobe. "The only section of wall we haven't tested is behind that."

Olivia nodded. "I thought the first night that maybe the previous occupants shoved it there to block the passageway for privacy, but if it's blocking the passageway, then how could someone have gotten into the room?"

John crossed the room to the wardrobe and opened the doors wide. The wardrobe had drawers and shelves on one side and a hanging area for clothes on the other side. "A man could easily fit in here," John said, pointing to the side of the wardrobe with the rod. "Maybe he was already in the room and hid in the wardrobe when you came in."

Olivia shook her head. "I opened the wardrobe on the off chance there were clean linens. Besides, even if someone was hiding there, they had to get out. The windows and door were both locked from the inside."

John stared at the wardrobe and frowned. "Maybe the *wardrobe* is the passageway."

"Like a C. S. Lewis book?" Olivia said.

John stepped into the wardrobe and ran his fingers over the back panel, starting at the top. "I don't think it's a doorway to another world, but someone might have modified this wardrobe to cover the original opening."

He squatted and continued to search the panel at the bottom. In the right corner, he felt the

panel give a bit. He pressed the almost unnotice-able indention and the back of the wardrobe slid silently open, exposing a narrow passageway. He heard Olivia gasp behind him as he stared at the passageway in disbelief.

He'd known Olivia's idea was the only one that made sense, and he didn't believe she'd imag-ined the breeze in her room that first night. But thinking something could be real and seeing it in front of him were too different things—and opened an entire realm of possibilities that he hadn't considered before.

Possibilities that might lead him to his sister.

He poked his head into the passageway but couldn't see anything in the pitch black tunnel. The wardrobe barely allowed light across the threshold of the entry but the passageway ran the length of the room, allowing no illumination beyond the first foot of the opening.

"Hold on a sec," Olivia said, and he heard her rustling in the room behind him.

He turned to see what she was doing, and she stepped into the wardrobe doorway and handed him a spotlight. He raised his eyebrows at her and she shrugged.

"Do you really have to ask?"

He turned on the spotlight and stuck it in the

passageway. The woman had a point. If staying in large houses of horrors was a normal part of her job, she probably carried a more unusual set of business supplies than the average writer. He'd already been impressed with her tool set she'd brought to check the walls, complete with stethoscope. There was something to be said for a woman whose luggage included more tools and equipment than clothes.

He shone the light to the right of the opening, but there was only a wall. On the left the passageway extended about ten feet, then appeared to end. The entire passageway was maybe two feet wide and the ceiling was barely higher than his head. Servants back then must have been short and skinny.

"Well?" Olivia asked, poking her head into the tunnel.

"I can't tell if it turns at the end. I'm going to take a look."

"Be careful. The floorboards could be rotten or weak."

John shone the light down on the wooden pathway. Fresh, new lumber shone back at him. "Looks like someone kept this part of the house repaired." He took a couple of steps down the passageway.

"What the hell?" Olivia asked.

He glanced back as Olivia shone a flashlight on the repaired floor.

"Why in the world would someone make repairs here?"

John continued down the passage, checking each section of the wall for a possible sliding panel to an off-shooting tunnel. "I think if we had the answer to that question, we'd know who was sneaking around here and why."

"Do you see anything?"

"Not so far." He covered the last couple of feet in the passageway and frowned when he realized the wall simply stopped, rather than turning as he'd hoped. He knocked and pressed on the end wall, hoping to find some way to make it shift or open but it didn't budge. "I don't understand. It's a dead end." He looked back at Olivia. "You seem to know some about the architecture of these homes. Do you want to take a look?"

Olivia bit her lip and stared at him.

"Is something wrong?" he asked.

"No, yes…it's just that I'm a little claustrophobic."

"You're kidding me. With your job?"

"I don't write in closets," Olivia shot back. "Give me a second." She took a single step into the tunnel, took a deep breath, then slowly blew it out. She inched down the tunnel toward him

and after what seemed like forever, finally stood behind him.

She placed one hand on his shoulder and peered around him at the solid wood wall. "There's got to be a way around it. Whoever replaced that flooring did it for a reason. Did you feel the edges for a release?" She pointed up at the corner of the passage end. "What's that?"

He looked at the corner. "I don't see anything."

"There's something shiny up there. On the framing at the top corner."

John shone his light up in the corner. "I don't see anything."

"My flashlight caught it for a moment. Turn your light off and let me see if I can get it again."

John turned off the spotlight and eighty percent of the illumination left the tunnel. He heard Olivia suck in a breath, then she shined her flashlight at the corner, slowly moving the light across the studs. Suddenly, she stopped.

"There," she said. "Where the bracing comes down at an angle in the top corner. Do you see?"

John looked up and saw a glint of something where the two studs met. He reached into the corner and felt lightly with his fingertips, just in

case it was something sharp. But whatever was shining was small and smooth and connected to some sort of fuzzy material. "It's metal."

"Could it be a release?"

"No. It's not attached to the wall and there is some sort of material attached to it. Hold on." He balanced the object between his fingers, careful to get a good grip, and carefully removed it from the corner.

"What is it?" Olivia asked, her ragged breathing giving away how hard it was for her to stand there.

John looked down at the object in his palm. "Some sort of bag with a shiny clasp on top. I'm not sure."

"Let's go back into the room and take a look."

John managed to turn around in the narrow space and followed Olivia out of the tunnel and back into the master suite. He opened his hand to show her the object as soon as he stepped out of the tunnel. Olivia's eyes widened as she stared at the black velvet pouch with a metal clasp. John opened the clasp and turned the pouch upside down, dumping a tiny bit of gold jewelry onto his palm.

Olivia took one look at the object and gasped. A bolt of lightning broke across the sky and the

lights went out, pitching the room into complete darkness. As he struggled to find the switch on the spotlight Olivia staggered backward, and he dropped the light and caught her with one arm before she fell. He could feel her heart pounding against his chest as he clutched her warm body against his. The honey-sweet smell of her hair flooded his nostrils and his body began to respond in entirely inappropriate ways, now or ever.

He released her slowly, making certain she wasn't going to collapse, and retrieved the spotlight from the floor. He pressed the switch and the room flooded with light. Olivia slumped onto the end of the bed, clutching her flashlight and staring at his hand as if the object was going to leap up from his palm and attack her.

John took in her flushed face, ragged breath and shocked expression. He narrowed his eyes at her. "I think it's time you and I have a talk about exactly why you're here."

Chapter Six

Olivia sipped on her cup of tea and looked across the kitchen table at John. A lantern on the table cast a dim glow in the room, causing shadows to dance on the walls like the night creatures in some of her stories. She struggled to get control of herself, but her hands shook as she placed the cup back on the table.

"Thanks for the tea," she said. "I'm sorry I freaked out on you. You've been really patient, but I know I owe you an explanation." She opened a small plastic container she'd brought with her from the bedroom. A container that she never traveled without.

"Everything I know about my past is in this box," she said.

"I don't understand."

"I was raised in an orphanage. All the nuns could tell me was a woman left me there one night in the middle of a thunderstorm. I was only a year old. The woman said she couldn't

be responsible for what would happen to me and begged them to take me."

"Did they call the police?"

"Yes. The police issued a statement to the public asking for people to report anyone who used to have a baby but didn't any longer and gave a limited description of the woman. It was dark and she wore a hooded jacket, so the nuns couldn't provide the police with much to go on."

"But no one ever came forward."

"No. They finally assumed the woman wasn't from the area, which is why no one had identified her. Since I was safe with the nuns, no one felt the need to escalate it to a national level, so I stayed at the orphanage with the nuns."

"They didn't try to get you adopted? I would think someone would be interested in a baby so young."

Olivia stared down at her tea, knowing she needed to tell John everything, but she doubted he'd believe her. No one else did. "I was placed a couple of times, but both ended badly so the nuns didn't try again."

"Ended badly?"

"The nuns said I would scream like I was being murdered and wake everyone up from a dead sleep. Nothing they did would soothe me.

It took hours for me to calm down. The nuns had me checked repeatedly by doctors, but they couldn't find anything wrong."

"But obviously it stopped."

"No. I just stopped screaming."

John's eyes widened. "What causes it?"

"A dream. I've had it as long as I can remember. Sometimes once a month, sometimes every night, but it's always the same."

"Can you tell me about it?"

Olivia blew out a breath. "I don't want to, but I think I have to. I need someone to tell me I'm not crazy or paranoid."

John nodded, but Olivia noticed he didn't make any promises.

Olivia took a deep breath and began. "It starts off like I'm flying over a wooded area. I swoop down into a clearing and approach an enormous house. I fly inside an upstairs window and then the dream shifts. I'm in a bed sleeping. It's a large room and the bed is ornate with tall pillars on each corner and gauze draped around it. A man walks into the bedroom and stands next to the bed, staring down at me. Even though I'm asleep in my dream, I can see him standing there almost as if I'm also floating above the bed."

Olivia took another drink of her tea and focused on staying calm. "As I open my eyes, he

raises a dagger above me and plunges it into my heart. I can see his eyes as clearly as I see yours now. They're completely dead, and I know he doesn't feel an ounce of remorse for what he's done. I gasp for air, but I can feel my lungs collapsing, my heart beating so loudly that it drowns out all the nighttime noise. I clutch my chest and scream, trying to drown out the sound of my fading heartbeat. Then I wake up."

"Do you recognize the man?"

"No. In my dream, I know that I know him, but when I'm awake, I can't remember his face. Only his eyes."

John hesitated for a moment and Olivia could tell he was struggling for the right thing to say. "I'm sorry you have to deal with that, and it sounds truly horrifying, but I don't understand what it has to do with your being here."

Olivia pulled a small jewelry case out of the container and opened it. She held the case across the table for John to see. "This is the other half of the locket you took from the tunnel. I was clutching it when the nuns took me."

John stared at the two broken pieces, and Olivia could tell he desperately wanted another explanation, an easy, risk-free answer. "I'm sure there was more than one locket made. I admit,

it's a startling coincidence, but I think you might be reaching."

Olivia shook her head. "That locket was not mass produced. I took my half for appraisal. The jeweler said it was handcrafted and about one hundred and fifty years old. I'd bet anything that if we take both pieces to a jeweler, he'll say they're a match."

"So maybe someone followed you here. Someone who's always had the other half and for some reason is choosing now to try and freak you out. This situation still has all the makings of a stalker."

"Maybe, but I don't think so."

"Why not?"

"Because this is the house from my dreams."

John's eyes widened.

"And that woman in the photo—the one that looks like me," Olivia continued, "was murdered by her husband."

JOHN GLANCED OVER AT THE COUCH in the caretaker's cottage, but even with the dim light of the lantern he could see Olivia was out cold, probably from sheer exhaustion. Wavy locks, the color of caramel, fell across her forehead and rested on her perfectly-defined cheekbones. Even in her sleep Olivia's face had that timeless

beauty to it, just like Marilyn Borque. She hadn't even argued when John had suggested she stay at his place that night, which meant she'd either seen the logic behind leaving a place where no room was necessarily secure, or she'd simply been scared to death. Maybe both.

Not that he blamed her.

The entire situation was more bizarre than what he was used to, and Olivia had every right to be scared and upset. The situation disturbed him on so many levels, he was having trouble wrapping his mind around them all. He stared out the kitchen window at the sheets of rain and sighed. The last thing he needed was to take anything else on right now, but it didn't look like he had a choice. Like it or not, Olivia might be the key to unlocking the secrets of the house and finding his sister.

John didn't buy into some past life dream transference, and he could tell Olivia was skeptical as well, but the reality was that some very strange things had happened and at the moment neither of them had a logical explanation. The only thing he was certain about was that someone, a living breathing someone, was laying a trap for Olivia with the photos and the jewelry. Someone who wanted to remain hidden in the shadows but someone with an agenda.

What John needed was more information—about the house and Olivia, but after she'd delivered that last statement about the murdered woman it was clear her defenses and emotions were crumbling fast. He needed information, but he needed her thinking clearly when she gave it. So instead, he'd offered her a glass of wine and a safe place on his couch and planned to question her again first thing in the morning. They couldn't afford to waste much time.

John had two theories based on what Olivia had told him, but neither were much more credible than a vision in a dream. The first theory was that Olivia had been to the house as an infant. The second theory was that her biological mother or someone close to her, maybe a foster parent, had been murdered and Olivia had seen it. Even though she'd been a baby, maybe something had been impressed on her memory. Something that came back to her in her dreams.

He blew out a breath and shook his head. If that didn't sound like an *X-Files* episode, he didn't know what did.

Regardless, all signs pointed to something big whirling around Olivia Markham—something even Olivia didn't have a grasp on. John wondered exactly what his sister had had the misfortune to step in the middle of. Whatever

it was, the intruder probably hadn't counted on an extra person in the mix, and assuming his sister had come across this person, what had he done to her? John could only hope that whatever the intruder's ultimate plan may be that it didn't include murder.

He'd hoped the camera Olivia had found would give him proof that his sister had been at laMalediction, but he'd only found pictures of the exterior of the house and a couple of shots of the entryway. They were definitely things his sister would have taken pictures of for her thesis, but it couldn't be considered concrete proof. Frustrated, he rose from the table and pulled a beer from the refrigerator.

He should be inspecting the attic or trying to figure out where that tunnel was supposed to lead, but he didn't want to leave Olivia alone. The photo on Olivia's bed was proof the intruder was escalating, and as soon as John got a chance he needed to dust the photo and the tunnel switches for prints. Leaving that photo was brazen, even with the tunnels, in the middle of the day and with both of them right there in the house.

Then there was the flip side—if the intruder had his sister, the best way to get to him was through Olivia. He felt a moment of guilt that

he was using her, but he pushed it aside. He might be using her, but in doing so he was also protecting her.

At least that's what he was telling himself.

OLIVIA FLEW OVER THE SWAMP surrounding laMalediction. She knew she was dreaming, but no matter how hard she tried she couldn't force herself awake. It was the same as before, the storm, the outline of the house, and she clenched her eyes, trying to block out what she knew she'd see but everything remained in full view. This time she hovered in front of the house and Olivia saw Franklin Borque pass in front of the window in the formal living room.

She dipped down and the view changed, almost as if she were peering into the house from the outside wall. Franklin Bourque was in the kitchen, opening one of the cabinet drawers. He was wearing dinner clothes, but Olivia somehow knew it was the middle of the night. He pulled something from the drawer, but his body blocked the object from Olivia's vision.

When he turned, the blade of the knife flashed in the light of the lone candle on the kitchen table, and Olivia sucked in a breath. He looked down at the blade, turning the knife over and over in his palm. He smiled as he looked at it,

his eyes flashing wildly with excitement and anticipation. He drew the blade of the knife across his open palm and blood spilled from the cut. He brought his palm up to his face and licked it, smearing blood across his jaw.

Olivia knew for certain that he was mad.

He walked up the stairs, blood dripping from his cut hand, the knife clenched in the other. The door to the master bedroom was closed and he didn't even attempt to open it. Instead he continued past it several feet, then pressed his hand on the wall, leaving a bloody handprint on the white plaster surface. A section of the wall slid back and Olivia realized he was entering the passage that led to the master bedroom from the hallway.

The dream shifted immediately to the inside of the master bedroom and Olivia expected to be in the bed, but this time the dream changed and she hovered above the bed watching the scene play out below. Marilyn Borque lay sleeping in the bed, completely unaware of the danger in the hallway. The wall where the wardrobe now stood was bare and Olivia watched as the panel slid back and Franklin Borque entered the room.

Olivia screamed at Marilyn, trying to wake her from her deep sleep, but no sound came out. Her throat burned as she struggled to make a

noise, and she felt her lungs would explode as Franklin stood above Marilyn and thrust the knife deep into her heart.

The sound of tearing flesh freed her throttled voice and her screams finally broke free. She bolted upright in a panic at her unfamiliar surroundings. Where the hell was she? Her vision blurred, and a second later someone grabbed her shoulders and shook them.

"Olivia, wake up!"

She gasped for air, clutching the fabric of the sofa, and finally remembered she was in the caretaker's cottage. Her vision began to clear and she saw John standing over her, felt his hands on her shoulders, his voice trying to bring her out of the nightmare. She took a deep breath and blew it out slowly, then lay back on the couch, trying to slow her racing heart.

John crouched beside her. "Was it the dream?"

Olivia nodded, not yet able to speak.

He placed his hand on her arm. "From your description last night I knew it had to be horrifying, but I have to tell you, you scared the hell out of me. Your scream was so primal, the fear so evident. And when I found you…your eyes were wide open, but it's like you couldn't see me. Like you were trapped in there."

"I was. That's the worst part. I know I'm dreaming but I can't wake myself up."

"Was this one the same as before?"

Olivia shook her head and told him about seeing Franklin Bourque in the kitchen. "He was mad, and I mean in a clinical sense. I could tell by his expression."

"You're not going to get any argument from me. Anyone who cuts open their own palm before murdering their wife clearly has issues." John frowned and stared at the wall behind her for a couple of seconds. "The dream has always been the same until now, right?"

"Always."

"So why do you think it changed now?"

Olivia rose to a sitting position and tucked her knees in front of her, encircling them with her arms. "Maybe being at the house? The house, the storm, even some of the furniture is the same."

John nodded. "Maybe so. Given your past, the horrific history of the house's residents and your imagination, it's not any wonder that your subconscious would whirl out of control with the stimulus it's received."

"But it seemed real. I know you find this hard to believe, and I'm not saying you aren't right in your assessment, but I think what I saw may be the truth."

"Are there any official records?"

"Yeah, but they're sketchy. Mostly, the police had only the servants' word to go on because Franklin died the same night."

"Of what?"

Olivia shook her head. "I don't know. I couldn't find anything on it, except that one of the servants walked for two days to get the police. Cypriere was no more than a village at the time. The police arrived to find Marilyn Borque stabbed to death and Franklin dead in the middle of the courtyard."

John frowned. "He died in the courtyard and the servants left him there for days?"

"People are superstitious in these parts. You know that. No one wanted to touch the body of 'the devil.'"

"And the police never determined cause of death?"

"Not that I could find. After the initial discovery the entire story just fell off the map as far as paperwork goes. It's like everyone wanted it to go away." Olivia took a deep breath and blew it out. "With everything I know about the murder, it could have happened exactly like my dream. Nothing in my dream contradicts the actual reports."

"Very slim reports," John pointed out. "I...I'm

sorry, but I can't go there. It's too far beyond what I believe. People who've been in horrendous situations often have issues with dreams. Like soldiers with post-traumatic stress disorder."

"But I've never seen a murder or anything else that traumatic. I think I would remember if I had. And how do you explain my seeing the house in my dreams before I'd ever been here? I don't pretend to have the answers, but I don't think you do either. I think somewhere between our two differing opinions lies the truth."

"Maybe, but all we have to work with now is reality." He rose from the floor. "It's almost dawn. I figure you have no intention of going back to sleep, so I'll make some coffee."

He stepped into the kitchen and started spooning coffee grounds into the coffeemaker. Olivia rose from the couch and headed for the bathroom. Maybe a dash of cold water on her face would help clear the fog from her mind. She was fully awake but her mind still felt cloudy, as if she was stuck in limbo between reality and her dream.

She closed the bathroom door and stared at herself in the mirror. The one thing she was certain of was that the dreams were no coincidence. Despite her talent for inventing spooky stories, she somehow knew that this story wasn't a

fabrication of her overactive imagination. Olivia was certain that somehow, she'd witnessed a murder that had happened over a century ago.

Ten minutes later, Olivia took a huge sip of coffee and avoided looking across the table at John. In the dim light of day, she felt foolish for her panic the night before and was mortified that not only had she slept on the couch of a man who was practically a stranger, but also she'd awakened him by screaming like a frightened child. Olivia had always avoided sharing personal information with others, especially men, but there was something about John that made her want to trust him. Which went against something else she'd always avoided—men.

"I've been thinking about the tunnel," John said.

"Yeah. What about it?"

"Well, obviously someone planned to use it or they wouldn't have made repairs."

Olivia nodded, even though the only reason someone would have for needing the tunnels was her occupancy of the house. "It's because of me, right? I mean, the house has been empty all these years, so no one would need a way to sneak around if I wasn't there."

"Based on everything that's happened, I have

to assume the intruder is here because of you. I may be wrong, but…"

"It would be a huge coincidence." Olivia shook her head. "I don't do huge coincidences, not even in my books. I know they happen, but not near as often as people might think. Usually there's someone with a motive."

John narrowed his eyes at her. "That sounds like something a cop would say."

Olivia shrugged. "I have to understand a lot of personality types to write good books, including the bad guys, and I spend a fair amount of time consulting with law enforcement as well as with behavioral analysts. Everyone's got a motive, John. Some of them are good, decent and altruistic, but there's always a reason behind what people do."

"Well, I'd prefer not to wait until the big showdown to figure out what this guy's motive is, so we need to come up with a plan."

"Okay, but where do we start? I don't think whoever put the picture in my room entered through the main hallway, like my dream. The walls there don't have plaster now, but wallpaper, which would show a seam. Besides which, if he was going to stroll through the house and up the stairs, why use a panel in the hallway when the door to the bedroom wasn't locked."

"I agree," John said. "There's nothing in the hall to indicate a panel still exists, assuming it ever did. Besides, the tunnel doesn't run the length of the bedroom wall. It stops short of the hallway by a good five feet."

Olivia sighed. "I need to go through those albums in the library and see if I can get more information on the Borques. You need to find the trip switch in the tunnel and figure out where all the entry points are, otherwise I'm sleeping in the kitchen pantry to be safe."

"And then there's the fact that both of us have real jobs to do, and I don't think we're making much progress." Olivia didn't even want to think about how far behind schedule she was on the book and no way was she notifying her editor.

"The maintenance can wait," John said. "I think your safety trumps repairs."

Olivia pursed her lips and thought for a moment. "What do you know about the previous caretaker?"

"Not much, really. Wheeler said he had a family emergency and had to take off for a while, but apparently Wheeler had been trying to hire more capable help before that."

"So he was already gone when you got here?"

"Yeah. Wheeler told me to use his cottage

until he got back, but said he didn't know when that would be."

"I wonder if someone repaired the floor in that tunnel before he left and if so, how did they manage without him noticing?"

John frowned. "I know he's old, and Wheeler said he was hard of hearing, but you're right. Someone would still have to haul lumber in here and cart it upstairs before they even began cutting and nailing. Hard to believe he could miss all that."

Olivia nodded. "I think we need to locate the old caretaker and ask him a few questions. It doesn't sound like Wheeler knows much of anything."

"No, it doesn't, but I can still call and ask."

"And say what?"

"I'll make something up. Pass me my cell phone."

"It's barely daylight."

"That didn't stop you from calling him yesterday. From where I sit, Wheeler has a fair amount to answer for. If he has to do it with the chickens, that's not my problem."

Olivia pushed John's cell phone across the table and he punched in Wheeler's number. Olivia hoped the attorney knew more than they

thought he did. The old caretaker might be able to clear everything up.

"Wheeler, this is John Landry at laMalediction."

Olivia perked up and waited for John to question Wheeler.

"No, everything's as expected given the lack of maintenance over the years, but I'm having some trouble locating breakers for some of the wiring in the main house. I wondered if you had a way I could contact the old caretaker for a quick chat about that and a couple of other things. It would save me a ton of time."

Olivia gave John a thumbs-up. At least his story was a plausible one.

John listened for a couple of seconds, then frowned. "So you have no idea how to reach him? Do you even know where he was going?" John looked over at Olivia and shook his head. "Well, I guess I'll make do without him. But if you happen to hear from him, would you please ask him to give me a call on my cell?"

John closed the phone. "Dead end. Wheeler says Aubrey, the old caretaker, didn't say where he was going, doesn't own a cell phone and he has nothing in his files on the man other than his name and social security number.

"Aubrey's probably been working at laMalediction longer than Wheeler has been alive. No

reason for him to dig into the man's business, I guess. So what now?"

"We could always take a trip to town and ask around."

Olivia frowned, not relishing a visit to the town that officially gave her the creeps. "Do you think they'll talk to us? I stopped at the café for directions on my way in and you would have thought I'd asked them to sacrifice their firstborn."

"They probably just don't like outsiders."

"I'm sure they don't, but it was more than that."

"What was it then?"

Olivia's mind played back her visit to the café. "They were skittish...uneasy." She looked John directly in the eyes. "It was like they were all afraid."

HE LOOKED DOWN at the caretaker's cottage from a tiny window in the attic tower. He'd left the photo hoping to hurry the woman along to her discovery...her destiny, but something had gone wrong. They'd found the tunnel entrance in her bedroom and that complicated everything, but he hadn't expected her to flee the house and hole up with the caretaker. Even the discovery

of the tunnel shouldn't have caused that much panic.

Something else had happened. Something he didn't know about and hadn't planned for. And that bothered him more than anything else.

The front door of the caretaker's cottage swung open and he watched expectantly as both of them stepped outside. She would come back into the house. She had to. It was written.

But instead of crossing the circular drive, they got into the caretaker's truck. He clenched his hands as they drove away from the estate. They didn't carry any luggage so they were likely only going to town, but this wouldn't do at all. There was no time to waste. The full moon was approaching. Three more days and Olivia Markham would fulfill the prophecy.

His life would be set. Hers would be cut short.

Chapter Seven

Huge droplets of rain began to fall from the gray sky as Olivia stepped out of John's truck and hurried across the street. Three men sitting in the corner of the otherwise empty café looked up as Olivia stepped inside, but all it took was a single glance for them to lower their eyes and lean forward to whisper across the table. John had suggested the cook might be more comfortable if she was alone, as the man had helped her before, so he'd gone to the gas station to pick up some supplies.

Olivia slid onto a stool at the counter and waited for the cook to plate some eggs and toast and deliver it to one of the men in the corner. The man spoke to the cook and the cook glanced at her before shaking his head and saying something to the man that made the entire table frown.

The cook headed back to the counter and gave her a nod. "I guess you made it all right?"

"Yes, thank you so much for the directions. I missed the twisted trees on the first pass, but your map was great."

"No problem. Coffee?"

"Please, and the breakfast special. I've been living on protein bars and peanut butter sandwiches."

The cook broke a couple of eggs on the grill and slid bread into the toaster. "So you haven't changed your mind about staying there?" he asked, but he kept his gaze directed away from her.

"Not until I'm finished with my book."

The cook placed a full cup of coffee in front of her, and Olivia took a second to breathe in the strong aroma. Rather than immediately moving away, the cook stood there and studied her.

"Doesn't it make you nervous?" he asked.

"No," Olivia lied, and realized that was the first time her answer to that particular question was a lie. "I'm used to it by now. I live in a different house for every book."

"Probably ain't seen anything like laMalediction, though. Place is cursed."

Olivia nodded. "It's that sort of rumor that makes it a great place for a story."

The cook's eyes darted to the men in the corner, then back at Olivia and he shook his

head. "The things that happen at laMalediction ain't no story in a book. Place ain't safe, if you ask me."

Olivia mentally cheered. The cook had given her exactly the opening she'd been looking for. "It *is* very run down. I'm careful when I use the stairwell or walk in the upstairs rooms, to check the flooring first. The lights don't work in a large section of the house. I figure there's a breaker tripped, but I haven't been able to locate the box."

The cook narrowed his eyes at her. "Aubrey's lived there his whole life. How come he won't fix it?"

"Is Aubrey the old caretaker?"

"If you mean old, as in age, yeah, he's ancient."

"No, I meant he's not there now. The estate attorney said he had a family emergency and sent a new guy to cover for a while. But he's been so busy with damage from the storm that he doesn't have time to mess with the lights. He figures I should make do with the other parts of the house until he can get to it."

"Family emergency?" The cook frowned. "I don't recall hearing anything about that." He turned back to the grill to plate her food.

"Maybe it came up at the last minute," Olivia

suggested. "I wish I knew where to find him. A simple phone call would probably save me an afternoon of hunting around in the basement. Part of the section without lights is the library and I want to dig through the books and family albums for research." Olivia gave herself a mental pat on the back for the lies that rolled off her tongue.

The cook turned and slid the plate in front of her. He rubbed his jaw with one hand, his brow wrinkled in concentration. "Best I know, Aubrey's family is all in Johnson's Bayou, a little town a couple of hours west of here. I don't know any of them, but the family name is Murphy."

Olivia smiled. "Thanks! I'll try looking them up."

The cook frowned. "Thing is, though, I could swear I saw Aubrey's truck driving through town last night."

Olivia stared. "What time?"

"Late, after the storm started. I was still up here hassling with a broken gas line on this grill. Guess I could have been mistaken. It was still storming and there ain't no streetlights to speak of."

Olivia shrugged, trying not to let on how much the cook's words interested her. "Well, he sure hasn't been to the house. But I'll see if I can get

in touch with him today and get those lights working. I really appreciate the help."

The cook nodded and glanced at the men at the corner table. Olivia could barely see them from where she sat, but she could tell they'd stopped talking as soon as she'd started and were likely hanging on every word. That didn't seem to please the cook at all.

"My name's Olivia, by the way," she said and extended her hand across the counter. The cook hesitantly shook it. "I was in such a hurry to beat the storm the other day that I don't even think I introduced myself."

"I'm Tom Breaux. I own this café."

"It's nice to meet you, Tom." Olivia glanced at the men in the corner, leaned across the counter, and lowered her voice. "Can I ask you a question?"

"Yeah," Tom said, nervously. "I guess so."

"Why does my staying at laMalediction seem to bother people?"

Tom's eyes widened. "Surely, you know about the house. I mean, that smooth-talking attorney didn't con you into thinking it was safe there, did he?"

"I know the house's history, if that's what you mean."

"Then you know that people who go there

rarely come out unless it's with the coroner. Aubrey's the only person that's been to la Malediction in my lifetime that ever came back out."

Olivia's heart skipped a beat and she forced herself to sound normal. "Are you saying other people have died there besides the original owners?"

Tom nodded. "Couple of surveyors a few years ago was poking around, said they had to measure the bayou or something foolish. I figure they was really trying to see if the land held oil, then they'd try to pick it up for a song."

"What happened to them?"

"The sheriff tried to keep it all hushed, so as not to scare people, but I heard the rumors all the same. Those two men shot each other. Ain't no one got a reason why. But my friend Billy works for the doctor two towns over and he drove the bodies to the morgue. He unzipped the body bags and took a peek."

Olivia stared at Tom, not even blinking. "What did he see?"

Tom glanced at the men in the corner and leaned further across the counter, his voice a whisper. "He said their faces looked like they'd been scared to death."

Olivia fought the urge to cross her arms across her chest. "Wow. You're right. That is a

scary story. Are they the only ones you know about?"

Tom nodded. "The only ones they had bodies for, but every couple of years or so, someone comes into town wanting to poke around the house. I see 'em come into town, but I never see 'em leave."

"Maybe they leave when you're at home or busy."

"Maybe. Or maybe they're still at that house. Maybe the reason the lights don't work is they're trying to speak to you. Trying to warn you, even."

Olivia studied the man's face, but she saw no slyness in his expression. Whatever was going on at laMalediction, it was clear by the expression on Tom's face that he believed it was malevolent. "I'm careful because I know it's in bad need of repair," Olivia said, "but it's just a house. There's nothing evil about it."

She saw him clench his jaw, and he leaned toward her, staring her straight in the eyes. "No, ma'am, that's where you're wrong. I'm not given to fanciful things, but the truth is, there's more things in these bayous that can't be explained than can. I know deep in my bones that pile of stone and wood is not *just* a house. Somewhere

between 'nothing' and those stories you write is the truth."

Olivia felt the hair rise on the back of her neck as Tom turned and began scraping the grill. What did it take to make a grown, strong, able-bodied, seemingly sane man that intense over a structure of stone and wood? Maybe if Tom had been sequestered here his entire life she'd get it, but she recognized the military tattoos on his arms. Tom was no backwoods hick who'd never crossed the parish line.

But he still believed in monsters.

JOHN STEPPED INTO THE DOORWAY of the library and paused when he saw Olivia looking out the window, talking on her phone. She turned to face the doorway and waved him inside, frowning as she thanked whoever was on the phone and disconnected. "Any luck?" he asked.

Olivia shook her head. "None of Aubrey's relatives has seen him in years, much less in the past couple of days."

"Any other relatives we don't know about?"

"According to his niece, the family in Johnson's Bayou is all Aubrey has left."

"Girlfriend?" John suggested, but he knew it was a stretch. Hard for a man who'd been se-

questered at laMalediction for eighty years to find a girlfriend.

"No chance. His niece said women irritated him and made him paranoid. Apparently, he thinks we all have ulterior motives."

"Don't you?"

"Motives, yes. Ulterior, depends on the woman." She dropped into a leather chair and looked up at John. "This missing caretaker thing…it's that coincidence dance all over again." She sighed. "I don't buy it."

John shook his head and slid into the chair across the table from her. "I don't, either. There's simply too many things at play and none of them add up."

Olivia bit her lower lip then asked, "What do you think happened to him?"

"I have two guesses. Either he had a run-in with our intruder…"

"Or?"

"Or he *is* our intruder."

Olivia's eyes widened. "You really think so?"

"Yeah. Considering he told Wheeler he had to leave for a family emergency but none of his family is aware of an emergency, it looks like he lied. He wanted people to believe he'd left laMalediction."

"That makes sense, and would explain why Tom Breaux saw his truck last night. Even if he was old and slow, he'd still know every square inch of the house including the secret passages."

John nodded. "And he wouldn't have to hide the passage repairs from himself."

"But how is he getting back and forth from wherever he's hiding?"

"Maybe he never left the house," John suggested.

"Then why did Tom Breaux see his truck?"

"Maybe he was mistaken."

Olivia frowned. "Maybe. But let's just assume Tom Breaux wasn't mistaken and it was Aubrey's truck. That means he's driving to and from somewhere, and he's certainly not driving up the main road and parking in the front drive."

"No, he's not, but God only knows how many trails run through these woods. And if anyone would know an alternate route to laMalediction, it would be Aubrey."

John pointed to Olivia's laptop. "You got internet on that thing?"

Olivia held up her satellite phone attached by a cord to the laptop. "Yes."

"Then pull up Google maps and see if we can

get a satellite view of the area. If the alternate route isn't covered completely by the trees we might be able to see it."

Olivia smiled, pulled up Google maps and typed in the town of Cypriere. "I don't know why I didn't think of this. I pulled up Google maps of the house before coming here and didn't even think about it. And I'm supposed to be good at research."

John pulled a chair over next to her and watched the screen as an aerial view of Cypriere developed. Olivia could feel the heat coming off of his body, but instead of making her nervous it made her feel safe until she thought about it in that vein and then *that* made her nervous. Depending on other people wasn't a weakness Olivia had ever had, and was one she couldn't afford to develop. Depending on hot, strong men all alone in the middle of nowhere was just asking for trouble.

She lifted her arm up a tiny bit, just so his forearm was no longer touching her, and clicked the mouse to select a satellite view. She zoomed in on the area a couple of times, then pointed to a hazy set of buildings. "There's the town. This house is east and maybe a little south, right?"

John leaned in further to study the screen and

his forearm touched hers again. "That sounds right."

Olivia clicked the mouse a couple of more times, shifting the satellite image southeast until they saw a large clearing in the forest. "That's it," Olivia said, pointing to the roof of the main house.

John stared at the screen and frowned.

"What's wrong?" Olivia asked.

"You said you looked this up before coming here, but you didn't know it was the house in your dreams before arriving."

"I know. I think it's because in my dream I'm flying toward the front of the house and into the window. Just seeing the top of the roof wasn't enough to trigger anything with me. But from the front of the house, you can see all the gables and the stained glass."

John nodded. "A matter of perspective." He pointed to a winding line on the west side of the estate. "That's the main road and even that doesn't show. The Cypress trees really have it covered, and it's hazy. It must have been raining when the satellite took the shot."

"There's a shocker." Olivia inspected the tiny line that appeared intermittently on the screen, then scanned the woods surrounding the home hoping to spot something similar. "What's that

north of the house, in the woods behind the caretaker's cottage?" Olivia pointed to a miniscule break in the trees some distance behind the cottage.

John studied the screen and pointed above her finger. "Yeah. Look at this break a little farther north. It could be a road buried back there. Move the satellite view farther north."

Olivia clicked the mouse and the screen shifted to expose a larger area of woods and marshland north of the estate. "There." She pointed to a thin, curving line. "It looks like it runs to a river."

"Bayou," John corrected. "It isn't big enough to be a river, but southern Louisiana is full of bayous and channels. Zoom in on the bayou north of where we saw the path."

Olivia zoomed in as far as the satellite photo allowed. "It's roofs. Do people live there?"

"Probably. And some that have houses elsewhere keep another place on bayous to fish. They call them camps, but a lot of them are little more than shacks that would crumple in a high wind."

Olivia scanned the photo surrounding the camps. "I don't see any roads to the camps. Just the barest traces of a trail from laMalediction."

"They probably get there by boat."

Olivia sat back in her chair. "Great. So we can be attacked by land or water, and since everyone in this town probably owns a boat, then we haven't exactly narrowed things down."

"Not exactly. But whoever owns those camps would be our best bet for someone who knows about a path to laMalediction."

Olivia nodded. "So what do you want to do?"

"You got any hiking boots and a raincoat in one of those boxes?"

Olivia smiled. "As a matter of fact, I do."

Chapter Eight

It took almost an hour of stomping through the dense brush behind the caretaker's cottage before they located something that could barely serve as a pathway for a vehicle. It was about a hundred yards behind the caretaker's cottage and there was no way someone in the main house could see anyone approaching from that direction.

John glanced at his watch. "Even though the rain stopped, it's still really overcast. We've got a couple of hours before we start losing light, maybe less because of the trees."

Olivia pushed the hood of her rain jacket back and wiped sweat from her forehead. "Assuming this takes us to those camps, how far do you think it is?"

"A couple of miles maybe. It's hard to tell from the satellite map, especially if the path winds a lot."

Olivia nodded. "Then I guess we best get moving."

John gave her the once-over, and Olivia hoped the exhaustion she was beginning to feel didn't show. "You sure you're up to this? Even though it's fall, the humidity here gets to people who aren't used to it."

"It will be humid again tomorrow and I want to know what's going on."

"Then let's make tracks. I don't want to get caught out here after dark." He turned and started down the path, disappearing as he rounded a corner in the brush.

Olivia set out beside him, trying not to think about the things John had left unsaid. The dense brush and gray sky had already choked half of the light out of the swamp. The glow of the moon wouldn't even scratch the surface. *I don't want to get caught out here after dark*. But it wasn't the dark that they had to be afraid of. It was the creatures that hunted in the dark and this marsh was probably full of them.

Not to mention whoever was trying to scare her. Olivia was pretty sure she didn't want to run into him in the dark, either, even with her pistol tucked in the waistband of her jeans.

Olivia walked silently beside John, carefully observing the terrain before she took a step. The last thing she needed was a sprained ankle

when the nearest doctor was probably light years away.

It took forty-five minutes to reach an abrupt end to the path, a giant wall of brush. John pointed to a muddy area just behind the brush. It looked like branches had been dragged through the mud. "Someone thinks he's being clever."

"He *is* clever. Who knows how long they've gotten away with using this path."

"Let's find a way around this mess. I want to leave it intact and try not to step in the open muddy area. I don't want to leave footprints for him to discover."

Olivia nodded and followed John around the side of the brush, careful to place her feet on dense undergrowth. They picked up the path on the other side of the brush and followed it another five minutes when suddenly John crouched behind a bush, pulling Olivia down with him. He placed one finger over his lips and pointed. Olivia peered through the brush and realized they were directly behind the camps from the satellite photo, and someone was approaching in a boat.

Olivia peered through the branches and tried to make out the man as the boat pulled up to the pier, but he had a cap pulled low and he was looking down as he docked the boat. He tied the

boat to a pylon, then grabbed a box from the boat and placed it on the pier. When he rose all the way up with the box, Olivia placed her hand on John's arm and squeezed.

"That's the cook," she whispered. "Tom Breaux."

"You're sure?"

"Positive." Olivia looked back toward the pier and watched as Tom placed two more boxes on the pier. "I can't make out the writing on the side of the boxes."

"Too far away," John agreed.

They watched as Tom stepped onto the pier and picked up one of the boxes. He headed toward the middle of the three camps and set the box on the steps next to the back door, then repeated the process for the other two boxes. After setting the last box on the top of the pile, he knocked on the back door and it opened. Olivia narrowed her eyes, trying to make out the figure inside the camp but it was dark and she didn't have a clear view.

The door to the camp opened and Tom carried the boxes insides, one by one. Ten minutes later, he stepped outside and started back toward the dock. In the branches of the tree above their hiding place, a hawk cried out and took off, breaking a branch off the tree with his launch.

Tom stopped short at the sound of the breaking branch and looked directly at their hiding place. Olivia released the branches and ducked further down behind the bush, almost colliding heads with John as he ducked as well. Even though she knew he couldn't hear her breathing from that distance, she sucked in a breath and held it, praying that Tom wouldn't decide to take a closer look.

The seconds ticked away like hours and Olivia focused on an ant crawling across the top of her hand. She felt John shift beside her and he tapped her on the shoulder. "He's leaving," John said.

Olivia straightened back up to a crouch, releasing the breath she'd been holding out with a whoosh. She peered through the bush just in time to see Tom start the boat and back away from the dock. She turned to face John and was suddenly aware of the proximity of their bodies. "What do you think?" she asked as she tried to shift backwards and increase the inches between them.

John stared at her for a moment then looked back at the bayou. He rose from the hiding spot and shook his head. "I don't know. Could be it's his place. Could be he was delivering to some-

one. I didn't get a look at whoever opened the door."

Olivia rose to stand beside him. "I didn't either. It could be a man or woman or Bigfoot for all I could see." She scanned the area surrounding the camps. "I don't see any vehicles here, though."

"No, but someone could easily navigate the path with an ATV. One would fit in that storage shed over there with no problem."

"Do you think we should try to look inside?"

John scanned the camps, and Olivia could tell his mind was processing the pros and cons. "No, it's too risky," he finally said. "And wouldn't prove anything except that someone has access to laMalediction, which we already know. It wouldn't tell us if that person is Tom or Aubrey or someone else completely."

Olivia nodded. "I don't see another road."

"Yeah, I noticed that. You can probably only get to these camps by boat."

Olivia shoved her hands in her pockets and looked up at John. "I don't like it. Tom basically warned me away from the house, insinuating that it made people die or disappear, and he's the one who claimed he'd seen Aubrey's truck

driving through town, but he's got a pathway to laMalediction in his backyard."

"If the camp is his."

"Yet another coincidence?"

John frowned.

Olivia opened her mouth to continue, but John clamped his hand over it. Instinctively, she started to struggle, but then realized he was looking back toward the camps.

"It's Tom again," John whispered. "He's docked his boat and is coming this way...with a shotgun." He grabbed her hand and pulled her off the path and into the dense foliage of the swamp as he began to run.

Olivia lurched forward at his tug and then broke out into a run behind him. Branches slapped against her face, slinging rainwater into her eyes and causing her vision to blur. Her thighs burned with the effort of running through the dense brush wearing the heavy hiking boots. John was about ten feet ahead of her, but he glanced back every couple of seconds to make sure she was still behind him. Olivia could hear Tom tearing through the brush behind her, so she knew he was in pursuit, and from the noise level, it sounded like he was getting closer by the minute.

For a split second, she worried they were

running the wrong way. The cypress trees seemed to close in, confusing her sense of direction. What if they'd veered too far off the path and got lost in the swamp? She was just about to pull her pistol from her waistband and prepare for the worst, when they broke out of the swamp and into the lawn just to the east of the storage shed near the caretaker's cottage.

John made a dash for the shed and slipped inside, leaving the door open. Olivia reached to close it, but John put his hand out to stop her. "It's better if he thinks we're working. That it wasn't us he was chasing."

John handed her a set of safety glasses and a pair of welding gloves, then grabbed the chain saw and headed out of the shack. "Take a couple of deep breaths and act normal," he whispered.

"I appreciate your help with this," John said in his regular voice as they left the storage shed. "I hope I didn't interrupt your work."

"No." Olivia waved a hand in dismissal, trying her best to appear nonchalant. She couldn't see Tom anywhere, but she would swear she could feel him watching. "I needed a break and sometimes physical activity is the best way to loosen the creative mind."

"Really?" John smiled. "Then prepare to have

your mind well loosened. I'd like to get the rest of that tree cleared out of the drive before it gets dark. The rain got me a little behind." He stopped in front of the tree and pointed to her welding gloves which she slipped on. "Grab the other side of this branch."

Olivia stooped down to wrap her arms around the thick branch. John bent over at the other end of the branch, his head just inches from her. "He's in the brush just behind the storage shed," he whispered without raising his head to look at her.

Olivia took a deep breath and fought the urge to look over at the storage shed.

"Ready?" John asked out loud.

Olivia nodded and they lifted the branch and carried it over to the pile John had started just outside the driveway. On the way back to the downed tree, John said in a low voice, "He's gone."

"Are you sure?"

"No, but he's not standing where he was before."

"So what's the plan? If Tom's our intruder then he could easily slip into the main house and watch us the rest of the day, and we can't stay out here all afternoon just to throw him off track."

John motioned to the end of another thick branch. "Lift your end, then drop it," he said in a low voice. "Grab your wrist like you hurt it."

Olivia nodded and lifted her end of the branch. She took one step backward and lost her grip. She pretended to stumble, then let out a cry and grabbed her wrist with her other hand. John immediately dropped his end of the log and rushed over to her. He told her to hold out her wrist and he slipped off the welding glove, pretending to inspect her wrist.

"Good job," he whispered, then in his regular voice said, "You need to clean this and then I'll help you wrap it." He motioned toward the cottage. It had only one entrance and that had been in John's sight the entire time. "I've got supplies in the cottage. Go ahead and get it cleaned. I'll put the tools up and be right in."

John picked up the chain saw and her gloves and headed for the storage shed. Olivia left the drive, trying to walk at a normal pace even though her body was practically crying to break out into a run. It seemed like forever, but she finally slipped into the caretaker's cottage and closed the door behind her. She leaned back against the door and slowly slid to the floor, her heart still pounding.

JOHN PLACED THE CHAIN SAW and gloves back on a shelf in the storage shed and pulled the door closed behind him. He'd scanned the brush as he walked toward the caretaker's cottage, trying to make out any movement or color that didn't belong, but everything was silent. The optimist in him wanted to believe they'd fooled the cook with their little stunt, but if Tom Breaux was the intruder, the realist in him didn't think it worked.

If anything, their act might have made things worse because they'd alerted the man that they were onto him and trying to play games. Lack of respect was an insult to people who were a little off mentally, and John didn't think for a moment that someone sneaking through tunnels to leave creepy old photos on the bed of strange women was the least bit sane.

Which made him worry about his half sister even more. If she'd come to laMalediction like her calendar indicated, then it was very likely she'd stepped right into the middle of something very strange. And from the looks of it, dangerous. Whatever was going on, he needed to figure it out fast, before things got worse. He'd managed to dust the tunnel for prints that morning while Olivia was working in the library, but the only prints were his own. He had no doubt the

photo would be the same, and couldn't help but remember that Tom Breaux had been wearing gloves when he unloaded those boxes and chased them through the swamp.

John blew out a breath. He was getting in deep with Olivia and the mystery surrounding the estate. He kept telling himself that his sister was somehow mixed up in all of this—that solving Olivia's problem would ultimately lead him to his half sister, but was he just fooling himself? He couldn't deny that Olivia brought out feelings in him that he usually kept repressed. His mother and sister were enough responsibility for one man, and John had no intention of adding to the mix. But he couldn't deny that he found her interesting, both mentally and physically. She would be a hard woman to ignore even under normal circumstances.

He stepped into the caretaker's cottage and closed the door behind him. Olivia was in the living room, peering between the slats of the blinds. "You see anything?" he asked.

"Nothing." She turned to face him. "What about you? Did you see him when you were putting the tools away?"

"No," he said.

"So do you think it worked?"

John blew out a breath, not wanting to share

all of his thoughts on the matter, especially as they'd probably only scare her more. "I don't know. I'd like to think so, but we fled fast. I don't know if we left footprints."

"Oh, no." Olivia covered her mouth with her hand. "I didn't even think about leaving footprints. It has to be him, right? I mean, why else would he chase us?"

John shook his head. "For a million other reasons I can think of, just off the top of my head. A lot of illegal activity goes on in these swamps. Drug deals, arms trading and a host of other activities. If Tom was mixed up in something illegal delivering those boxes, and he thought something was out of order, he would check it out."

"He was running after us with a shotgun," Olivia pointed out.

"That's one way of checking things out on the bayou."

Olivia threw her hands in the air. "What now? If we assume it's the caretaker, he's got the advantage of home turf. If we assume it's the cook, he's got a way in and a loaded gun, and a bunch of creepy stories to scare everyone else away. We're at a disadvantage either way. They've both had years to learn everything about this swamp

and the house. How can we possibly combat that?"

"One of the first things we can do is figure out where the tunnels run in the house. We can't keep him from approaching laMalediction through the swamp, but we need to cut off his method of movement through the house."

"I didn't even ask you if you had any luck with the bedroom tunnel this afternoon."

John shook his head, knowing his frustration was showing. "No. For the life of me, I can't figure out how to go beyond that wall at the end. There has to be another opening, but everything seems solid—sounds that way, too."

"There's no reason to build a tunnel to nowhere and even less of a reason to repair it. There has to be an opening somewhere."

"I don't suppose…no, never mind." The last thing he needed was Olivia taking more risks.

Olivia bit her lower lip. "You want me to take a look at the tunnel."

"Forget it. I don't want you to do anything that makes you uncomfortable. I'll figure it out. It's just a matter of time." Time he didn't really have.

Olivia shook her head. "Don't waste time coddling me. If you need me to look at the tunnel, I will. Since whatever is going on seems to center

around me, the least I can do is help solve my own problems."

John felt a wave of relief, then admiration pass over him. Despite a dramatic night of personal revelations and an all-too-recent brush with death, Olivia was still willing to take chances. "I rigged your spotlight at the top of the tunnel entrance this morning so I could work without having to hold a light. It's pretty bright in there if that makes a difference."

"Yes, it does. In the dark things seem closer. It makes the claustrophobia worse."

"Okay. When do you want to do this?"

"No time like the present."

A wave of relief washed over John that Olivia wasn't going to delay entering the tunnel. With her knowledge of old homes, she might be the key to unlocking whatever secret the tunnel held and ultimately the secret to what might have happened to his half sister.

They exited the caretaker's cottage and crossed the courtyard to the main house. John scanned the brush as they walked, but didn't see anything that indicated they were being watched. In the main house, he headed upstairs to the master suite, Olivia trailing behind.

He turned on the spotlight and illuminated the tunnel, then handed Olivia a smaller flashlight.

It wasn't really needed with the spotlight, but he figured holding the light in her hands would help keep Olivia from panicking in the closed space. Olivia stepped into the wardrobe and poked her head inside the tunnel, then leaned back, took a deep breath and stepped into the tunnel.

"I'm going to talk while I look, okay?" Olivia asked. "Talking helps keep my anxiety down."

John stepped into the wardrobe and peered into the tunnel. "Whatever you need to do. Why don't you tell me about the history of these tunnels."

Olivia stood just inside the tunnel and shined her flashlight on the back wall, then began pressing the surface with her fingers. "In the old days, the wealthy believed servants shouldn't be seen, so they built these passageways so the servants could move throughout the house performing their regular duties without disrupting houseguests or the master and mistress of the house."

"Sounds sorta rude, and vain."

Olivia let out a short laugh, but John could tell it was forced. "It was rude, and vain, but they lived in a different time and were expected to live as other wealthy people dictated. It probably saved the servants a lot of grief, if you think about it. You can hardly be accused of scuffing

a marble floor you don't walk on or ruining a rug by spilling drinks, when the only way you traverse the house is out of sight."

"Maybe, but I'm sure they got blamed for everything anyway."

"Cynic." Olivia took a couple of steps more down the tunnel and started her analysis of the next piece of wall. "But you're probably right."

She stopped working on the wall for a moment and looked back at John, frowning.

"What's wrong?"

"I was just thinking that I'm wasting my time with these sides. There's no reason to design a tunnel this long unless the other doorway is at the end. I mean, there may be another offshoot, but why extend something to nowhere?"

"That makes sense, but I checked every square inch of the walls at the end of that tunnel. They're solid. I would swear to it. No hollow sound at all."

Olivia stared at him for a moment. "Maybe it's not the walls." She walked to the back of the tunnel and shined her flashlight on the ceiling.

"Do you want me to help?" John asked.

"No. You would block the light, and it would make the tunnel feel smaller."

"Are you calling me fat?" John asked, trying

to take Olivia's focus away from the narrow space she occupied.

She laughed this time for real. "Hardly. If you have an ounce of fat on you, it's probably in your head."

John smiled, pleased to know that she'd noticed him that way. "There are a lot of people who would probably agree with that assessment."

Olivia shot him a grin as she felt across the ceiling with her fingers. She paused when her fingers reached the corner. "This feels different. It has some give."

"Be careful."

"What's the worst that can happen—another panel slides open?" She pressed her fingers into the ceiling and John heard a single click, then the floor beneath her dropped.

Chapter Nine

He ran into the tunnel, but before he could reach her she was gone and the floor had closed. "Olivia!" he yelled, but there was no reply. Panicked, he stood back from the end of the tunnel and reached forward, pressing the ceiling where Olivia had been working. He located the trip switch and pressed it.

The floor in front of him slid back, and he looked into the hole. "Olivia!"

"John!" she yelled back.

John felt relief wash over him, even though they weren't out of the woods. "Are you all right?"

"I think so. The lift sorta dropped at the very end, and I twisted my ankle whcn I fell off, but I'm okay."

"Do you have your flashlight? You need to get back on the lift and figure out a way to get it up."

"I dropped it but I think I felt it with my foot. Hold on."

John heard shuffling and then Olivia's voice came back, sounding more strained. "It's broken."

"Don't panic," John said and rushed to the tunnel entry and yanked down the spotlight. He hurried back to the opening and shined the spotlight down the hole, then drew in a breath when he realized exactly how far down Olivia was. It was at least a thirty-foot drop. "Don't look up," he instructed her, "or you'll blind yourself. But see if you can find a release to send the lift back up."

He watched as she stepped onto the lift and could tell she was favoring her left ankle. She felt the walls around and then she stopped. "I think there's a problem," she said, her voice shaky.

"What is it?"

"It's a broken cable. That's why the lift seemed to crash at the end."

John blew out a breath and tried to think. "Can you see another way out? The lift has to go somewhere."

"The light doesn't go much beyond the lift. I could try feeling my way."

"No. We have no way of knowing what's down there. You could end up injured."

"How far down am I? It felt like a long drop."

John hesitated for a second, not wanting Olivia to know just how closed in she was.

"John?"

"About thirty feet."

"Oh."

That single word said it all. John knew he had to get her out of there, and fast. He'd heard horror stories of claustrophobics who had died of a heart attack when they were closed in. And there was also the chance that Olivia wasn't down there alone. "Olivia, I need to set the light down for a couple of seconds. I promise it won't be long, but I need you to be still, okay?"

"Okay."

John hurried to the tunnel opening and removed the strap he'd used to secure the spotlight to the ceiling. He rushed back to the opening and shined the spotlight into the hole. "I'm back. I'm going to secure the spotlight to the ceiling above the opening so that I don't have to hold it. Give me another couple of seconds, okay?"

"Yeah."

John shoved the strap through a ceiling beam, concerned with the one-word answers and the weak sound in Olivia's voice. He secured the strap through the handle of the spotlight and

tied it into place. "Okay, the light is secure. Are you all right?"

"I'm okay."

"I need you to take deep breaths. I'm going to get you out of there."

"How?"

John felt his heart clench at the scared but hopeful sound in her voice. "There's a long rope in the storage shed. I'm going to get it and lower you a light. That way you can find another exit. You have to be somewhere in the basement. Once you have a light, I'll go down to the basement and see if I can help from there."

John waited a couple of seconds, but there was no answer. "Olivia? Did you hear me?"

"Promise me you'll come back."

"I promise. Nothing in the world can keep me away, okay? I should only be gone about five minutes. I'll be right back." John rushed out of the tunnel and ran down the stairs and out of the house. Stupid, stupid, stupid. He'd put her in that hole. Risked her life to find his sister, and as much as he wanted to find his sister, what he'd done wasn't fair or right. But he was going to fix that, now.

And hope she didn't have a nervous breakdown before he made things right.

OLIVIA SAT ON THE LIFT, her knees pressed against her chest with her arms surrounding them. She struggled to control her breathing, to keep from panicking. This was her nightmare—stuck in a small space with no way out. Thank God for the floodlight, otherwise she'd probably lose her mind. She lifted the leg of her jeans a bit and looked at her ankle. She could already see the swelling. It didn't feel broken, but if she was being honest, she didn't really feel it at all over her beating heart.

It's only a couple more minutes.

Surely, John had been gone for a few minutes already. He would be back anytime now. Soon. With a rope and a plan. She checked her watch and was horrified to realize barely a minute had passed. She tapped the face of the watch, wondering if it had stopped working but in her heart she knew it hadn't.

She stared ahead of her, straining to make out something, anything, but not a ray of light illuminated her surroundings. She could be sitting in a closet or a performance hall for all she knew. If only she hadn't dropped her flashlight on the way down. She couldn't help but wonder if the intruder was somewhere in the house. If so, she was a sitting duck.

She took a deep breath and slowly blew it out. Pulling at a frayed spot on her jeans, she wondered if she should sing or count backwards from a thousand, something for a distraction. Then she heard a noise above her.

"John?" she called out, overwhelmed with relief. Her watch had been wrong. John was back and he was going to get her out of here. She waited a couple of seconds, but he never answered. She felt her heart drop, realizing she must have imagined the noise.

Until she heard it again.

"John! John, if that's you, please answer!" She held her breath, trying to make out the noise, and was certain she heard rustling above her.

Then everything went black.

She screamed and clenched her hands so hard she felt her fingernails dig into her palms. Sweat broke out immediately on her forehead and her palms and she swayed dizzily, unable to center herself in the pitch-black. What if it had all been a trick? What if John's intention from the beginning was to trap her in the basement and leave her there?

Sure, he couldn't be responsible for all the things that had happened, but how did she know he wasn't working with someone else? For all

she knew, the intruder and John could be in on everything together.

Stop it!

Olivia tried to gain control of her racing mind and focus on the truth. Unless he's the best actor in the world, the panic in his voice after she fell on the lift was real. John was the good guy, but he was obviously not alone in the house, and the intruder knew exactly where she was.

Trapped.

If the drop was thirty feet, that meant she was in the basement. The lift must have been a laundry chute, which meant the tunnel probably led to the laundry area in the basement. Olivia took a deep breath and rose to her hands and knees. Damned if she was going to sit and wait for him to come get her. She was going out fighting, even if she had to do it crawling.

She inched forward, feeling the floor beneath her before placing her body weight on it. The stone floor of the tunnel was cold and clammy beneath her hands, making her want to yank her hands back, but she had to be careful. The last thing she wanted was another surprise drop. She reached out to her sides and felt brick walls about four feet apart. Like a hallway, she told herself, trying to put the word "tunnel" and all its connotations out of her mind.

She passed her hand lightly over the floor in front of her to make sure no sharp objects could pierce her; then she pressed harder, ensuring the floor was solid; and finally, she felt the walls on both sides of her to make sure there was no door or that the hallway didn't shoot off in another direction. Not that she had any idea what to do if that happened.

She grew dizzy again and realized she was holding her breath. She let out the old air and drew in a deep breath, the stale air causing her to cough. Her heart beat like a metronome on high speed as she inched through the darkness. One beat, two beats, three beats. She found herself counting and moving to the rhythm.

And then she hit a brick wall, literally.

She felt the wall in front of her then felt to the sides again. It was a dead end. Both sides were completely encased in brick. Like a tomb.

She shook her head and struggled to redirect her mind. A dead end made no sense. Someone had used the tunnel so there had to be an opening. It was just a matter of finding the trip switch. A brick wall could move, right? She'd seen it in the movies, and of course, everyone knew that if you saw it in the movies it must be true.

She let out a sharp laugh. If she could still

manage sarcasm, she must not be as bad off as she thought. Rising from the floor, she tried to place the majority of her body weight on her good ankle. She felt the walls as she rose, trying to locate the trigger that would provide an exit. The brick was smooth and cold with patches of fuzzy growth that Olivia didn't even want to think about. The place was probably teeming with spiders. She absolutely hated spiders.

Concentrate.

She ran her hands across the wall, pressing, feeling, looking for the way out. Her heartbeat seemed to increase with every pass of her hands across the brick, and she felt the panic stirring in her stomach, the anxiety moving up her body like a slow burn. When she reached the top of the wall she sucked in a breath, trying to regain control.

It was too late.

Her heart pounded like it would leap out of her chest. Each beat sent a rush of blood to her head and she leaned against the wall, trying to steady herself. This couldn't be happening. Not like this. No one should have to die in their own personal nightmare.

Then anger, despair and fear overwhelmed her and she began to pound on the brick wall, screaming the entire time.

Chapter Ten

John tore open the door to the storage shed and grabbed a coil of rope from a shelf on the back wall, then ran back to the main house, hoping to God that the length of rope was long enough to reach Olivia. And that Olivia hadn't panicked. He took the stairs two at a time, each step pounding out an echo through the house. He ran into the wardrobe and stopped short in the pitch-black.

What had happened to the floodlight?

He stepped back into the bedroom and lit the lantern on the nightstand, then dashed into the tunnel, his heart pounding so hard it made his temples throb. He lifted the lantern at the end of the tunnel, but the floodlight was nowhere to be seen. He lowered the lantern and saw the false floor was back in place, closing Olivia off completely.

Panicked, he pressed the trip switch on the ceiling and the floor panel slid silently back.

He held the lantern into the opening, cursing when the light exposed only a couple of feet into the inky black. "Olivia! Olivia, can you hear me?"

But no one answered. "Olivia!" He strained to make out a noise, anything that might indicate she was still there and still breathing but the silence was deafening. He took a deep breath and tried to think. The bottom of the lift had to be in the basement. He needed to look in the basement.

He left the tunnel and studied the wall in the bedroom, estimating the length from the front wall of the house to the lift in the tunnel was about twenty feet. Based on his assessment of the second floor rooms the day before, he figured the tunnel was thirty to forty feet from the west wall of the house. He pulled his pistol from his ankle holster and checked it, then slipped it into the back of his jeans. That floodlight hadn't removed itself, and if he ran into whoever was playing games they were going to get a long look at the short end of a gun.

He rushed down the stairs and into the kitchen where the entry for the basement was located. At the bottom of the basement stairs, he flipped the light switch to illuminate the cavernous space. It only took a second to get his bearings, then

he hurried across the basement to a laundry area. The area was separated from the rest of the basement with a partial wall and the lights were out in the entire section. John had noticed it when working in the basement the day before, but hadn't thought much of it. Now he wished he had.

He held the lantern close to the wall, scanning every inch of it with his eyes and free hand. This had to be it. His calculation of where the chute dropped was correct. But he found nothing to indicate an opening. Damn it. The desire to punch his fist straight through the brick wall was overwhelming and he struggled to get his raging emotions under control.

He had to think. He had to think quickly and accu-rately.

Looking back at the basement stairs, he assessed the distance once more but couldn't find anything off from his original assessment. It was here. It had to be. Desperation overwhelming him, he lifted a loose brick from the ground and was just about to smash it into the wall when he heard something. He froze, certain he was imagining things, but it was still there. It was faint, but he could hear a woman screaming.

Olivia!

He stepped out of the laundry area and

followed the brick wall down the middle of the basement. The screaming was still faint, but he could tell he was closing in on her location. He held the lantern close to the wall, scanning the surface as he walked and then he drew up short. *There.* The screams were behind this section of the wall.

He set the lantern on the ground and ran his hands across the wall. Her screaming made his heart clutch, but at the same time gave him some relief that she was still alive and he knew where to find her. He could only hope she wouldn't be mentally damaged beyond repair.

He passed his hands over the brick wall a second time, then he felt it. A brick that gave ever so slightly. He pressed it and the entire wall slid silently back, spilling Olivia out of the darkness and into his arms.

OLIVIA CLOSED HER EYES, blocking off the glare of the lantern, and clutched John, unwilling to let go. She struggled to catch her breath, but her anxiety had taken over, making breathing hard. John stroked her hair and hugged her close to him.

"You're safe now," he whispered. "I am so sorry."

"The light went out. I thought it was all a trick.

That you'd tricked me into the tunnel to leave me there."

"God, no. Olivia, I would never hurt you! You have to believe me. But when I find who did…"

Olivia loosened her hold on him enough to look up. "I heard someone in the tunnel above me. He was there, John."

"I know. He took the light and closed the trap door in the tunnel." John looked down at her, the lingering panic and overwhelming relief clear in his expression. "Are you all right? Your ankle?"

"I twisted it a bit, but I think it's fine. I'm fine. I called out, but no one answered. Then everything went black. I started crawling, feeling my way down the tunnel until I came to the end. I tried to find a release but couldn't. I couldn't find it. Then I panicked. I thought it was all over."

John shook his head. "You are one tough cookie. Tougher than most of the men I know, and that's saying a lot."

Olivia dropped her gaze to John's chest. "I was on the verge of a heart attack. I'm not tough."

John put one finger under her chin and lifted her face up, looking her straight in the eyes. "You were confronted with your worst fear in a house that's been in your nightmares for as long

as you can remember, and you were still collected enough to find your way down the tunnel to the exit. You're incredible, Olivia."

He stared at her for a moment, the indecision on his face clear as day, and that's when Olivia realized he was going to kiss her. Her heart leapt into her throat as he lowered his lips to her, kissing her softly, his lips barely brushing her own. Her skin tingled everywhere their bodies touched. She leaned into him, the heat radiating from him making her feel warm and secure. The kiss deepened and her skin, previously cold from fear, began to tingle and warm from desire.

Suddenly, he broke away and took a step back. "I'm sorry. I didn't mean to…"

He stared at her, his expression filled with both surprise and fear. "We should get out of here and see to your ankle," he said. "And I think it's time we call the sheriff."

Olivia watched as he crossed the basement and started up the stairs. Her body was screaming for him to come back and finish what he'd started, but her mind knew it wasn't a good idea. How very interesting. If she was a betting woman, she'd bet anything that John was more afraid of that one little kiss than she'd been locked in that tunnel.

OLIVIA SAT SIDEWAYS at the kitchen table across from the sheriff, her foot propped up on another chair. Once they'd decided it wasn't broken, John had carefully wrapped her ankle after calling the sheriff. He'd halfheartedly tried to talk her into seeing a doctor, but both of them knew the nearest doctor with any sort of equipment was probably hours away and not worth the trip for what was probably a sprain.

John paced the kitchen in front of the table, clearly unhappy with the sheriff's stance on the situation at laMalediction. Sheriff Blanchard jotted down a couple of things on a notepad and looked across the table at her. "I understand how frightening that must have been, Ms. Markham, but you need to be more careful. Investigating secret tunnels like you're Nancy Drew in a house that hasn't had good upkeep in decades is just inviting trouble."

Olivia bristled at the condescending tone and held one hand up to stop John, who was either about to speak or clock the man. "While I appreciate that my trip down the laundry chute wouldn't have happened if I hadn't been doing research for my book, unless 'Trouble' lives nearby and wanted a spotlight, I don't think my snooping is the problem here."

Sheriff Blanchard looked up at John, who was

glaring down at him. "You sure you left the spotlight? I could see where in a panic, you mighta took it with you and forgot."

Olivia saw John's jaw twitch. "I did *not* take the light with me," John said. "Even panic doesn't mean one becomes an imbecile."

"Now, there's no cause to get riled," Sheriff Blanchard said. "I'm sure there's a logical explanation for it all."

"So am I," Olivia agreed. "And I'd like you to see to locking up that logical explanation. This is not the first time I've found evidence that someone was in this house besides me or John. I'm not crazy, Sheriff, and I want your word that you will look into this."

Sheriff Blanchard glanced up at John, then back at her, his expression a mixture of resignation and aggravation. "I'll ask around, of course, but it was probably kids. They'll sell that spotlight to a pawn shop up on the highway."

Olivia laughed. "Let me get this straight. This house is probably full of expensive antiques, and everyone in this town believes that if you set foot here, you'll die, but you think kids broke in here to steal my spotlight?"

Sheriff Blanchard frowned, clearly not used to logic being used against him. "Well, now, I'm not saying that's why they broke in, but if they

was already in the house and realized you was trapped in that laundry chute, then they mighta taken advantage of the situation and took the light both to make some money and scare you at the same time."

"And they would want to scare me, why, exactly? I was under the impression that the locals stayed away from this place altogether."

Sheriff Blanchard rose, apparently done with the conversation. "Most of the old-timers do, but kids ain't got no respect for tradition or lore."

"Or other people's property, apparently," John said.

Sheriff Blanchard narrowed his eyes. "There's no cause to start calling folk out. I'll give the kids a talkin' to if I find out who it was, but as there wasn't any real harm done, I can't do much else."

"I beg to differ," Olivia said. "I could have been seriously injured trying to get out of the tunnel and that spotlight cost over a hundred dollars, so I'll be expecting payment if you catch the kids that took it."

"I'll do what I can, Ms. Markham."

"Oh, and sheriff," Olivia said and he paused at the door to look back at her. "You might also want to pass on to the kids that trespassing is a crime. I'm licensed to carry a gun and I know

how to use it. I'm also well versed on my rights concerning breaking and entering in this state. I would hate for anything untoward to happen to some kids over a 'harmless' prank."

Spots of red rose up Sheriff Blanchard's neck and Olivia could see his jaw clench. He gave her a single nod and left.

"Pissed him off," John said.

"I intended to."

John looked down at her and frowned. "I'd bet everything it wasn't kids that took that spotlight."

Olivia sighed. "Me, too."

"Then why the parting shot about the gun?"

"Because I think Sheriff Blanchard knows who did it, or has a good idea, and I wanted him to warn whoever it is he suspects."

"If it's the same guy that left that picture, do you really think he'll stay away?"

"No. But when I shoot him, my butt will be covered."

John smiled. "I like your style. Just remember to make sure I'm clear before you fire."

"Based on the way you disarmed me my first night here, I doubt you're in much danger." She frowned. "Where did you learn that, anyway?"

John shrugged and looked away. "I just got lucky."

"No. It wasn't luck. I was as quiet as can be but you still knew exactly when I stepped into that doorway, even in the pitch-black."

"I grew up hunting. If you're going to hunt in the bayous and the swamps, you learn to be very quiet and listen really hard. Otherwise, that day of hunting may be your last on earth."

Olivia's mind flashed back to their dash through the swamp that morning. "I hadn't really thought of it that way. I guess you could hear me walking."

John nodded. "And breathing and when your body rubbed down the side of the wall. It was faint, but there." He looked out the kitchen window and blew out a breath. "I hate to mention this, but I see lightning in the distance. I think we're in for another big storm."

"Great. Another night with no power, trapped in a haunted house with an uninvited guest. If I had blond hair and big boobs, I'd be a living a cliché."

John laughed, then stared out the window and frowned. He was silent for a while, then looked back at Olivia, his expression serious. "I know we've already been over this, but maybe it's time you consider leaving. You could have

been seriously hurt today, and there was nothing I could have done to prevent it. We're behind the eight ball here."

Olivia nodded. "Like rats being forced through a maze. That's what it feels like."

"Someone was prepared for your arrival, Olivia. Someone who knows more about your past than you do, if those stunts with the photo and the locket are any indication. You can't get the best of an enemy when they're invisible."

"But how could he have been expecting me? Only my publisher and Wheeler know I rented this place."

"My guess is it leaked from Wheeler's office, probably a secretary or receptionist looking to make a quick buck. You have to understand, it's big news in these small towns—a famous author in a haunted house. Hell, I'm surprised it wasn't plastered across the front page of the *Times Picayune*."

Olivia sighed. "I guess so, but that still doesn't explain why someone would go out of their way to try and scare me. And no one could have known about my dreams. I've never told anyone until you. I mean, I think the nuns suspected, but they never knew exactly what was happening to me."

John shook his head. "I don't know what to

tell you. If it's all a big prank, then it's a huge coincidence that someone chose this house to try and scare you."

"And if it's not a prank?"

"Then we have to assume that someone has been waiting for you to come here. Someone who already knows about your connection to this house." He took a step closer to her and dropped one hand on her shoulder. "I don't want you to get hurt—any more than you already have been."

Olivia felt her chest tighten as she looked up at him. He was trying so hard to look stern and tough, but it was impossible to miss the care and worry in both his expression and tone. This man, a veritable stranger, had touched her in a way no other man ever had, and that both excited and scared her. Based on his retreat after kissing her, Olivia knew that John was just as confused by his feelings as she was.

Was she being fair to him? Staying at the house put pressure on him to take care of her, but regardless of feelings she wasn't his responsibility. Not to mention her remaining at the house might be putting him in danger.

"You're right," Olivia said finally, guilt getting the better of her. "But I can't do anything until

tomorrow at the earliest. I need to tear down and pack all my equipment."

John gave her shoulder a squeeze. "You shouldn't leave in the dark, anyway, and certainly not in a rainstorm. You want to be well clear of Cypriere in the daylight, on a clear day, that is."

"Yeah. I figured that one out the hard way."

"You'll stay in the caretaker's cottage tonight," John said. "It's easier to secure and I doubt there's a secret passage in all eight hundred square feet of it."

Olivia felt her heart leap at the thought of being in such close quarters all night with John. She'd been there the night before, but exhaustion had taken over, leaving no options but collapsing on his couch. But being locked up with him in a storm, probably with no lights, already aware that both their feelings were running high, made her edgy.

Leaving was definitely the right thing to do, before they did something both of them would regret. "Well, we still have power now. I'm not the fastest investigator in the world, with my limp, but I want to help while I'm still here and while we still have lights. Where do you want to start?"

John stared down at her, his indecision clear.

"I don't think it's a good idea for you to go poking around anymore."

"Probably not, but since you want to go poking around and you're not going to leave me here like a sitting duck I'm suggesting a compromise."

"Okay. The logical place to start is the basement. I want to reopen the tunnel you were trapped in and see if there are offshoots somewhere else. The dimensions of the basement are considerably smaller than that of the house."

"Really? Then there could be an entire maze of tunnels and rooms down there, hidden by stone walls."

"I know. That's what I'm afraid of."

Olivia shifted her propped leg onto the floor and turned in her chair to rise. John held onto her shoulder while she rose from the chair, steadying her as she stood. "You okay?"

Olivia placed her injured foot flat on the floor and shifted some of her body weight onto it, surprised when she felt only a small tingle of pain. "It's not bad. Much better than I thought it would be, actually." She walked across the kitchen to the basement door, careful to keep as much pressure off her injured foot as possible. John trailed closely behind her, apparently ready to intervene if she lost her balance.

"Good. It's probably only a light sprain, but

you need to be careful not to do more damage. I'll help you down the stairs. I want you to put as much of your weight as possible on me, okay?"

John opened the basement door and slipped his arm around Olivia's shoulders, pulling her tightly to him. Olivia felt the hard, muscular lines of his body press into her side and a flush started at her chest and crept up her neck.

Leaving was definitely the best thing to do—for both of them.

FROM HIS HIDING SPOT above them, the intruder listened to their conversation. He clenched his hands when the man suggested the woman leave. Surely, she wouldn't agree with all that he'd tempted her with. But she had agreed, and that just wouldn't do.

It was the caretaker's fault. He'd thought the caretaker had appeared at the property in order to help fulfill the prophecy. Why else would he appear out of nowhere after all these years? The spirits often sent others to aid, but maybe he'd been wrong. He was certain the woman wouldn't think of leaving if the caretaker didn't keep insisting. The caretaker had to go.

No matter what, Olivia could not be allowed to leave.

Chapter Eleven

Olivia shrugged off her dirty clothes and stepped into the steamy shower in the tiny bathroom of the caretaker's cottage. She sighed with pleasure as the hot water ran over her head and trailed down her body. She'd tromped through a swamp in the rain, been chased by a man with a gun, fallen two stories, twisted her ankle and been locked in a dark tunnel in a haunted house. It had definitely been a full day.

And then there was the kiss.

She poured shampoo into her hands and lathered up her hair, trying not to dwell on the kiss, especially while she was naked and wet. That was a recipe for disaster. She was leaving tomorrow. Thoughts of John Landry in the naked and wet position had no business in her mind.

She let out a sigh and stuck her head under the spray to rinse the shampoo. Who was she trying to fool? Ever since that kiss, she'd been more aware than before of how John affected

her. Even the brush of his arm brought her body alive in a way that she'd never felt before. It was a good thing she was leaving. Her feelings for John worried her almost as much as the hidden agenda of the mysterious intruder. Almost.

Even though she would have loved to have stood beneath the steamy water for an hour or two, she finished up her shower and grabbed a towel from the rack in the corner. John would need a shower, too, and there was only so much hot water in a tank.

As much as she hated it, she needed to email her editor and let her know she'd be packing up and moving once again. While the spa visit in New Orleans that her editor had recommended was tempting, Olivia knew it would be better for everyone if she got far away from Louisiana and whoever was having fun at her expense.

She wasn't even going to consider the possibility that the intruder would follow her.

JOHN PULLED HIS CELL PHONE from his pocket and glanced at the bathroom door. He waited to hear the shower start up, then pressed in the number for a friend in the precinct. The basement search had been a dead end. The laundry chute tunnel didn't have another access or take another direction that they could find, and they'd

been unable to locate another tunnel entrance before John had decided they had to give up for the night. Olivia was clearly exhausted and stressed and his own thinking was sketchy. He needed to regroup and come up with a plan.

"Fredericks," his friend answered.

"Brian, it's John. I need a favor."

"What the hell are you up to? The captain's been all over me like I know something."

Damn. "What have you told him?"

"Nothing. I don't know anything, and it sounds like that's a good thing."

"Well, you're about to know something. You know I wouldn't ask if it wasn't important."

Brian sighed. "The only thing that bothers me is that you didn't come to me earlier. You know I'll help you any way I can."

Gratitude and guilt washed over John like a tidal wave. He didn't deserve a friend like Brian. "It's not that I don't trust you. I didn't want you risking anything for me. You've already had enough trouble with the captain."

"Man, this is Rachel we're talking about, and your mom. You guys are like family."

"You're right. I shouldn't have left you out."

"I understand. What can I do to help, now?"

"I need you to do some digging on a sheriff in

Cypriere, name of Blanchard, and a café owner, Tom Breaux."

"Okay. You think they got something to do with Rachel?"

John gave his friend a brief rundown on the happenings at laMalediction and the earlier conversation with the sheriff. "I think he's lying, but I don't know about what."

"And the cook with the gun?"

"I don't know. Could be he's running something illegal through the bayous and it has nothing to do with this place. Could be he saw something and doesn't like people creeping around. Could be nothing."

"But might be something. I get you. I'll see what I can find out. Do you need me to come out there?"

"No. I need you back in New Orleans where you can check on things."

"Okay, man. I saw your mom after work today."

John felt his lower back tense. "How is she?"

"Upset, worried, exhausted. She said she hasn't heard from you since yesterday."

"Yeah, well, I've been a little busy. I'll call her later tonight unless I lose phone signal."

"Do that. Hey, what about that woman who's

renting the place? Seems sorta strange a woman wanting to stay at some creepy old house in the middle of nowhere. You want me to run down some information on her, too?"

John glanced at the bathroom door again, trying to block the mental image of Olivia in the shower from his mind. "No. She has nothing to do with Rachel."

"She's messed up in something though?"

"It looks like it."

"But she's not saying what."

"I don't think she knows," John said. "She's scared, and I get the impression that's not her norm."

"Maybe she knows more than she's letting on."

John bristled a little at Brian's words, but he knew his friend wasn't saying anything that he wouldn't have said had the situation been reversed. They were cops. They had to think that way. "She says she doesn't know and I believe her."

"What does she look like, this writer?"

"What's that got to do with anything?"

Brian chuckled. "Thought so. If she was an old hag, you would have described her straight out. Be careful, John. I know you've got good instincts, but you really don't know that woman,

and your emotions are already running high with Rachel missing. Even if that writer doesn't know what she's mixed up in, that house of cards could come crashing down on you, too."

John stared out the window at the rain, coming down in sheets. "I know. Call me when you get something, okay?" John closed his phone and tossed it onto the tiny table in the kitchen. He knew he should call his mother but he dreaded the conversation, knowing he couldn't lie to her even though he didn't want to tell her the truth.

He reached into his pocket and pulled out a silver charm bracelet—a bracelet he'd given Rachel for her birthday the year before. He'd discovered it when he and Olivia had searched the basement. It had been underneath an old table, just at the edge. A link was broken, which could mean nothing, but it could also mean that she'd hit her arm on the table or someone had manhandled her enough to break the bracelet. No matter the scenarios he could create, none of them were good. The bracelet proved Rachel had been in the house. Where was she now?

He needed to get back over to the main house and find out before the trail got any colder, but he needed to do it without Olivia. He blew out a breath. Looking for Rachel meant leaving Olivia

unprotected, pure and simple. He'd already seen the results of that once. Could he risk it again?

"What's wrong?" Olivia's voice sounded behind him.

He turned to face her, surprised he hadn't even heard her come out of the bathroom. She had on gray athletic shorts, a NY Yankees T-shirt and was towel-drying her hair, and damned if she still didn't look great. Brian was right. He was in trouble.

"The Yankees, huh?"

Olivia smiled. "It was a gift from my editor."

"That explains a lot."

"Really? Like what?"

"Like why someone locked you in a hole. He probably went through your luggage first."

Olivia laughed. "Ah, that whole Mason-Dixon thing. I didn't even think about it. I guess I figured an eighty-year-old caretaker and a house full of ghosts wouldn't care."

"Well, technically, Louisiana is more into football."

"Technically, so am I."

"Please don't tell me you like the Giants."

"Actually, I always kinda liked the Dolphins. I like the ocean."

"Now there's a unique method of choosing a favorite team." He glanced back out the

window at the main house. Did he run the risk or not? Now was the time. "I want to ask you something, but you have to say no if you're not comfortable."

Olivia gave him a wary look. "Okay?"

"I've been thinking about the intruder and how he gets around. I'd like to set up a trap in the basement."

"What kind of trap?"

"Nothing permanent, but tracking that sheet-rock all over the upstairs of the house yesterday gave me an idea. I could put some of the drywall dust from that ceiling collapse at the opening of the tunnel you were trapped in and at the bottom of the basement stairs. With any luck, the intruder will walk through it without noticing and give us an idea where another tunnel opening is hidden."

Olivia nodded. "It's a good idea, really. The lighting in the basement is so dim, no one would notice unless they look down. I mean, it's worth a shot anyway."

John blew out a breath of relief. "I'd need to do it now, before the storm gets worse. It's just starting up now."

"Sure. What's the problem?"

"I'm worried about you staying here alone."

Olivia waved a hand in dismissal. "I'm fine.

There's only one door into this place; I'm pretty sure and I can see every room from the kitchen table. I'll be right there working with a clear view of the front of the main house."

John studied her. The expression on her face was normal, but she pulled at the bottom of her T-shirt with one hand. She wasn't as comfortable with the situation as she wanted him to believe. He placed his hand on her arm, his fingers clasped gently around her soft skin. "Are you sure? Because I can do it tomorrow..."

"No. Then you lose the whole night, and he might come back tonight."

"Okay," John said and dropped his hand. He grabbed his jacket off the back of a kitchen chair and pulled it on while walking to the door. Olivia followed him to the doorway and put her hand on his shoulder before he slipped out.

"Be careful," she said.

John gave her a single nod and stepped out into the rain.

OLIVIA WATCHED as John crossed the courtyard and slipped into the main house. She crossed her arms in front of her chest as a shiver passed over her. Her damp hair must be giving her a chill. She sighed as she stepped away from the window and back into the bathroom. Even she

didn't believe that weak excuse, but at least she'd managed to fool John. Maybe. He hadn't exactly looked convinced when he left, but Olivia wanted him to go. If they could catch the intruder before she left, she might finally get the answers she'd been looking for all these years.

A quick glance around the tiny bathroom didn't reveal a hair dryer, but she wasn't surprised. John didn't exactly strike her as the primping sort of man. She grabbed a dry towel from a rack in the corner and wrapped it around her damp hair with a twist, then walked back into the kitchen. Her laptop was stuffed in her backpack along with the few other supplies she'd brought with her from the main house, so she pulled it out and set it on the kitchen table.

Staring out the window, she watched the drizzle that had been falling for an hour turn into heavy drops with wind gusts, seeming to blow in sheets across the courtyard. LaMalediction looked just like it did in her nightmare as she seemed to fly in from a distance. The jagged lines of the roof, the storm…the overwhelming feeling that something bad was about to happen.

Her nine millimeter was in the side pocket of her backpack and she pulled it out. She already knew the clip was full but checked it again.

Instead of slipping it back into her backpack, she sat it next to her laptop and slid into the chair at the end of the table. The one that offered a clear view of laMalediction.

She opened her laptop and pulled up the rough draft of her book, what little she had managed to write in between being stalked and trapped in small, dark places. Never in her career had a house made her so uneasy. Never had she spent so much time on edge, fear hovering just beneath the surface. Every emotion, whether it was fear or anger or attraction seemed to be magnified times ten. By all rights, she ought to be typing her best work ever, but instead she was wrapped up in a maze of secrets.

Sighing, she tried to focus on the document on her screen but images of John kept replaying through her mind. The relief on his face when she fell out of the tunnel and into his arms. The hesitation before he'd left her alone in the caretaker's cottage.

The fear in his eyes after he kissed her.

And ultimately, that was the clincher. John would investigate with her and protect her, but beyond that he'd drawn a line regardless of the obvious chemistry between them. Olivia didn't know whether to be relieved or disappointed.

Her body definitely wanted him and she could

hardly blame it, but her mind knew that even if she told herself it was just hot sex, she already felt more for John than was comfortable. While sex could sometimes be a welcome relief, Olivia instinctively knew that in this case it would just complicate everything, and more complication was something she definitely didn't need.

She forced herself to look at her rough draft, read the last paragraph she'd written and groaned. The independent, hardheaded heroine had just been rescued by the dark, mysterious hero.

Great.

JOHN SPREAD A THIN LAYER of Sheetrock dust at the bottom of the basement stairs, making sure he kept it in the area of the floor where the bottom step cast a shadow. With any luck the intruder wouldn't shine a light directly on the surface. Worst case, if he noticed, maybe he'd assume someone had spilled the detergent. John couldn't afford for the intruder to know they were trying to track him, especially when he had high hopes that the tracks would lead him to his sister.

He felt a momentary tug of guilt for continuing to mislead Olivia. He'd left her alone tonight claiming he was doing this for her, but his sister

was the primary reason he'd wanted to set a trap. If it had only been for Olivia he would have just caught the man and turned him over to the authorities, but he couldn't afford to do that given the situation with his sister. Too many crazies refused to tell where they'd stashed their victims and lots of times the time lost finding them was the difference between life and death.

And all that meant, in a way, that he was using Olivia as bait.

He gave the basement one final glance, then headed up the stairs to the kitchen. As he closed the basement door behind him, he heard the click of a door closing at the front of the house. He froze for a couple of seconds and listened, but heard nothing. Surely if Olivia had decided to leave the caretaker's cottage to find him she wouldn't be so quiet about it.

He turned off the kitchen light and waited until his eyes adjusted to the dark. He'd left the light on in the front entry and it cast a dim glow through the sitting room and into the kitchen entry. He moved silently across the kitchen and peered around the entryway. The sitting room and front entry were empty, and the front door was closed, but John knew he hadn't imagined the sound.

He slipped through the sitting room and into

the front entry, then peered out one of the narrow windows that framed the front door. The stained glass made it hard to decipher if anything was moving outside, and the blinding storm combined with meager outside lighting didn't help. He could barely make out the glow from the kitchen window in the caretaker's cottage.

Dual desires warred within him. He should go back to the cottage and make sure Olivia was protected, but he couldn't help feeling that he was missing an opportunity to investigate if the intruder was in the house right now. Finally he decided a quick scan of the downstairs wouldn't take that much time and he backed away from the window. That's when he noticed that the front door was unlocked.

He reached up and twisted the dead bolt, just to be certain, but he already knew before it clicked into place. The noise he'd heard wasn't someone coming into the house. It was someone leaving. He drew his pistol from the waistband of his jeans, opened the door a crack and scanned the circular drive. Stupid! He'd played right into the intruder's hands, leaving Olivia alone in the caretaker's cottage.

He eased out the door and stepped behind one of the huge columns that lined the front porch. The single light next to the front door barely

cast light beyond the porch, and he strained to scan the circular drive in the storm, barely able to even make out the cars parked in the drive. Pulling the hood of his jacket over his head, he decided to make a run for it.

The instant he stepped out from behind the column, he heard gunshots. He ducked down and whirled around behind the column again just as a bullet hit the column right above his head, scattering plaster with the blast. He didn't even have to assess the situation to know that he was screwed. The intruder had a clear shot at him and he had nowhere to run. Olivia's car was fifteen feet away in the circular drive and the front door, while only five feet from where he stood, was locked and had a light shining right above it.

At least one of the intruder's advantages had to go. Then maybe he could make it to Olivia's car. He edged around the column toward the house and pointed his pistol at the entry light next to the front door. He paused for a moment, knowing that as soon as he made the shot he had to be ready to run. Taking aim, he squeezed the trigger and took out the light in one shot.

The porch went immediately black, and he ran across the circular drive toward Olivia's car. He could hear gunfire, but couldn't tell the bullets'

path because of the rain and thunder. He was almost to the car when a burst of lightning lit up the driveway. A second later he heard a shot fire and felt a sharp pain, then a burn in his thigh. He dove behind Olivia's car, cursing the storm for exposing him at the absolute worst moment.

He glanced at the caretaker's cottage, but the twenty feet may as well have been a mile now that the intruder knew where he was. The situation had gone from worse to impossible.

Chapter Twelve

Olivia grabbed her pistol and dove out of her chair at the first sound of gunfire, then cursed herself for sitting right in front of the window. She crawled over to the wall and peered into the courtyard. The light from the front porch barely extended a couple of feet from the caretaker's cottage and the rain came down in sheets, never seeming to lessen.

She pulled the unraveled towel from the top of her head and tried to think. Could it have been thunder that she heard? But she knew better. She'd been to the shooting range so often that the sound of gunfire was ingrained in her mind.

Think, Olivia. What the hell is happening?

If someone had been trying to shoot her they should have succeeded, but they hadn't even hit the picture window she sat in front of. That could only mean that they were shooting at John. She stared into the blackness trying to make out movement, when the light at the main house

went out and the gunfire began again. She could barely make out a figure run from the porch and dive behind her car.

John.

She ran for the front door and threw it open, then turned off the porch light to mask her movement and slipped outside behind an old tractor, several feet from the entry. Another shot sounded across the courtyard and the driver's window on her car shattered. She peered over the tractor wheel, trying to determine where the shots were coming from. Based on the angle, it had to be from the far side of the courtyard, but where?

"John!" she yelled.

"Olivia?" John's voice sounded from behind her car.

Thank God. "I'm going to open fire. Run for it!" She laid her arms across the tractor wheel and squeezed off two rounds toward the far end of the courtyard nearest the main house, then directed her aim ten feet over from there and squeezed off another two rounds. She couldn't hear anything but the gunfire and the storm, and hoped that John was able to run. Aiming her pistol a little further down, she squeezed off another round before she felt a hand on her

shoulder pull her down just as a bullet grazed off the fender of the tractor with a zing.

"Get inside," John yelled above the storm and she lowered her weapon and ran back into the caretaker's cottage, John close behind. He slammed the door behind them, threw the dead bolt and pulled her into the bedroom at the back of the cottage. Only after he'd drawn the drapes did he slide onto the floor, his back against the bed, weapon still drawn, with a clear view of the front door.

Olivia slid down beside him, trying to assess his injuries by the dim glow of the bedroom lamp. He was soaked to the skin, which made things more difficult, but she sucked in a breath when she saw a dark circle at the thigh of his jeans. "John, you're hit," she said. "We have to get you help."

"It's just a scratch. The bullet grazed me."

"What the hell is going on here, John? It makes no sense."

"Maybe the sheriff asked some questions and let whoever locked you in that tunnel know you were armed."

"Then why didn't they shoot me? I was sitting at the kitchen table, the light on, in full view of anyone."

John stared at her for a couple of seconds. "I don't know."

Olivia blew out a breath. "Because he wasn't trying to shoot me, and you know it. You're just not saying it. If he wanted me dead, I would be right now, but instead, he came after you. Why?"

John ran one hand through his wet hair and Olivia could tell he was stalling. He had an idea, but he didn't want to share it with her.

"You know something," Olivia said.

John shook his head. "I don't know anything for sure."

"But you have an idea?"

"Yeah, I have an idea that whatever he wants from you, it requires you being alive. Based on the picture you discovered, I have to think it's personal, too, and that's the part that bothers me the most. A simple thief I could handle."

"But why go after you?"

"Maybe because he wants you alone."

Olivia felt a chill run through her at John's words. She'd known, deep down, that she was at the core of everything going on at laMalediction, but still couldn't wrap her mind around being the center of something she knew nothing about. It was unfathomable, but it *was*.

John rose from the floor. "I don't think he's

going to try anything with you in the house. He obviously needs you alive."

Olivia bit her lower lip and watched him head into the bathroom. She was putting him at risk. Just her presence at laMalediction was risking his life. There truly was no option any longer. She had to leave. Despite the overwhelming feeling that she was close to solving the mysteries of her past, she couldn't risk someone else's life to do it.

She rose from the floor to go see if he needed help dressing the wound. Tomorrow she'd leave the house and never return. She could disappear if she had to and her publisher would be perfectly willing to help, even if it meant getting her out of the country. At least long enough to find out what was going on.

John stood in the bathroom in front of the sink, inspecting the wound on his thigh through the torn patch on his jeans. "How bad is it?" Olivia asked.

"Not bad. I just need to dry it off and cover it. Even wet, it's barely bleeding."

"Why don't you take off your jeans and let me cover it?"

"I can get it."

"It's toward the back. I'll be able to reach it easier than you." She looked up at him. "What?

You think I've never seen a man in his underwear before?"

"How many men have you seen in their underwear with a gunshot wound?"

Olivia shrugged. "Okay, you got me there. This is definitely a first, and hopefully a last—the gunshot wound part, anyway. I'd sorta like to see a man in his underwear again before I die."

"Then I guess I'll accommodate you," John said and unfastened his jeans. Olivia reached for a clean towel on the rack behind him and watched as he carefully tugged the damp denim over his thigh and stepped out of the jeans. He pulled off his soaked T-shirt next and tossed it on the floor next to his jeans.

Olivia handed him the towel and tried not to notice the way the muscles in his abdomen rippled as he stretched to dry his back. He ran the towel down one long, muscular leg then the other, stopping short at the gunshot wound, which he patted gently.

"What do you think?" he asked.

Olivia's gaze flashed immediately from places it had no business being to his face. "I think you're perfect," was right on the tip of her tongue before she realized he was referring to the bullet wound. "Oh, uh, well let's see." She bent over to

inspect the wound, hoping he couldn't see the blush she felt creeping up her face.

She took a close look at the wound and reached for the cotton balls and peroxide he'd placed on the counter next to the sink. "It looks okay. Shallow, like you said. I'll clean it and bandage it so it doesn't rub against your jeans. Do you have any ointment?"

"There wasn't any in the cabinet that I could find."

"Wait here. I have some in my backpack." Olivia hurried into living room, then remembered her backpack was on the kitchen table— right in front of the picture window. She took a deep breath and dashed into the kitchen, snatched her bag from the table and rushed back into the bathroom. She took a deep breath as she placed the backpack on the counter next to the sink.

"You all right?" John asked.

"Yeah. My backpack was on the table in the kitchen, so I rushed."

John frowned. "You should have let me get it."

Olivia shook her head and pulled a tube of antibiotic cream out of her backpack. "How does that make sense if it's you he's after?" She fixed up a cotton ball with peroxide and dabbed it on the wound. "Does that hurt?"

"No."

Olivia held in a smile and kept cleaning the wound. Likely his leg could be completely severed and he'd swear it didn't hurt. John was definitely a man's man. "It's not deep," she said once she'd wiped away the blood. "I doubt it will even scar." *You'll still be perfect.*

She sighed and began to spread the cream on the wound, then covered it with a medium bandage to prevent chafing. When she rose, he turned to face her directly, their bodies as close as they could be without touching. She sucked in a breath as she felt the heat from his body on her own. She looked up at him expecting to see aggravation or impatience, but instead his amber eyes were fixed on her, the attraction undeniable.

She expected hesitation and retreat, but instead, he lowered his head and placed his lips on hers. Gone was the tenderness from earlier. Instead this kiss was urgent, hungry, and Olivia responded with the same energy, pressing her clothed body against his almost bare one. He stiffened slightly and Olivia thought for a moment he'd pull away again like he did before, but this time he gathered her in his arms and pulled her in closer.

Olivia wrapped her arms around him and ran

her hands down his back and across his rear end, like she'd been dying to do earlier. His body was hard and muscular, and she felt the heat in her rise as she imagined this man over her. *In* her.

He pressed his hips into her and she felt the long, hard length of him, only two thin layers of cotton separating them. She moaned and he lifted her from the floor and carried her into the bedroom. They stood at the end of the bed and he pulled her T-shirt over her head, exposing her bare breasts. He kissed her again, his hands caressing her breasts, his fingers circling around her nipples until she thought she would scream.

He pushed her cotton shorts over her hips and they slid to the floor. She dug her fingers into his back as he trailed kisses down her throat and took one engorged nipple into his mouth. His hand slid down her stomach and between her legs, his fingers stroking her where she ached for him the most. She pushed his briefs down and took the length of him in her hand and he shuddered. She stroked him with the same rhythm he used on her, back and forth, her hands moving across the smooth, hard skin.

She felt the climax build within her and cried out as wave after wave of pleasure rocked her body. He raised his head from her breast and

smiled at her, then lifted her up once again and placed her on the bed.

"Protection?" she asked. "If you don't have any, I do. Front pocket of my backpack."

He raised his eyebrows at her. "More supplies?"

"I like to be prepared for anything." Olivia grinned. "They've been there a while, though. I hope they haven't expired. That would be sad on so many levels."

John laughed and rose from the bed. "I'll check."

Olivia took a deep breath as he left the room, trying to absorb that she was about to sleep with a veritable stranger. Her mind flashed back to the way he felt in her hand and her already pleasured body throbbed for more. Hopefully those condoms were still good.

John walked back into the room, condom in hand. "You made it just under the wire." He lay down beside her and rolled the condom. He shifted over her and she parted her legs, allowing him to sink between them. When he entered her, she gasped and clutched his back, pulling him deeper inside her.

He set a smooth pace, their bodies and breathing in sync, and Olivia felt the pressure building in her again. His body stiffened and she felt her

pulse quicken, anticipating the release that was about to come. With a final thrust, he sent them both over the edge.

JOHN WAITED UNTIL THE CLIMAX subsided and kissed Olivia gently before sliding to the side, his arm still draped across her. His body was charged and sated all at the same time, reveling in a satisfaction he'd never felt before. This woman, Olivia, was different from the others before her, and John had no idea what to make of that. Especially now, with everything going on.

When his breathing became more normal, he pushed himself up on one elbow and looked down at her. She was beautiful—her hair tousled, her lips pink from kissing. Her eyes were closed and she wore nothing but a satisfied smile. John felt fortunate that he'd been the man to put that smile on her face, especially since she'd be leaving the next morning.

That bothered him, more than he wanted to admit, but it was the only way to keep Olivia safe and free him to look for his sister completely unencumbered by lies and misdirection. "So you really meant that whole 'preparedness' thing," he said.

Olivia looked up at him and smiled. "I never know when I might get lucky."

"The box hadn't even been opened."

Olivia waved a hand in dismissal. "Don't remind me. It's sad."

John laughed. "I guess it's hard to meet people with what you do."

"That, and then there's the fright factor. What I do tends to scare people away. They don't want to visit haunted houses and I don't stay in one place very long." Olivia raised one hand to stroke his face. "You know, I really hate wasting things. I bet we could use that whole box if we worked at it."

"In one night? I'm flattered, but even I have to admit I'm no superhero. Maybe when I was fifteen…"

Olivia's expression changed from playful to serious. "I don't have to leave. I mean, I know that's what we talked about, but I wonder if it's the best idea. I'm a good researcher, and I know a lot more about these houses than you. I could be a big help."

John's pulse quickened. This was a complication he didn't need. With Olivia safely out of the way he could concentrate all his effort on finding his sister. If she remained, he knew his loyalties would be divided. He looked at her—the earnest

expression with just a touch of excitement behind it. But was it for the thrill of the hunt or because of him?

Either way, he couldn't afford the liability. Making love to Olivia had been a huge mistake. It had shifted the playing field and created a situation he hadn't planned on dealing with. He had to convince her to leave, but he knew logical argument wasn't going to be enough. Olivia already knew the logic behind why she should leave. No, the only way she would budge now was if it was personal.

He rose from the bed and paced the length of the room. Olivia sat up on the bed and looked at him. "What's wrong?" she asked. "I thought you'd be happy to have my help."

John ran one hand through his hair. Now or never, Landry. "There's something you need to know about me."

"Okay."

"I'm not the person you think I am." He grabbed his wallet from the dresser and pulled out his badge. "I'm a cop—New Orleans Police Department."

Olivia stared at the badge, her confusion apparent, then looked back at John. "I don't understand. Are you investigating me?"

"No. I'm trying to find a missing girl. We

think she intended to visit laMalediction, but without proof that she was in Cypriere, Wheeler won't allow the police to search the property and we don't have the evidence to get a warrant to compel him to do so."

"You lied to Wheeler to get access to the estate?" Olivia frowned.

"It was the only way, and we're running out of time. The longer someone remains missing, the less likely they're ever found."

"And you lied to me," Olivia continued, "but what I don't understand is why."

John looked down at her, already hating himself for what he was about to say. "For all I know, you might have ratted me out. I couldn't afford to risk my job and the victim over someone I didn't know."

"Why would you risk your job for this girl?" Olivia jumped up from the bed, her hand over her mouth. "It's personal, isn't it? Oh, my God. It's your girlfriend. I just slept with some missing girl's boyfriend."

She closed her eyes and swayed, and for a moment John was afraid she was going to pass out. He rose from the bed and grabbed her shoulders with both hands to steady her. "It's not my girlfriend. It's my half sister."

Olivia opened her eyes and looked at him,

the disbelief still resident. "Then once you got to know me, why didn't you tell me? Surely, you know me better than to think I would get you fired and leave some poor woman trapped in this heap."

"I…I was afraid if I told you how dangerous I thought this place was, you'd leave."

Olivia stared at him for a moment, then her eyes widened and she pushed him away from her. "You *used* me. You knew someone was stalking me, and you hoped I would lead you to your sister. I guess having sex with me was the icing on the cake, right? Did you think I would be so wrapped up in you that I wouldn't care about all your lies?"

"Olivia—"

"You expected me to argue with you when you told me to leave this evening, didn't you? I must have ruined all your plans when I agreed to go, so you upped the stakes by having sex with me." She grabbed a spare blanket from the end of the bed and wrapped it around her. "Your days of using me are over. First thing tomorrow, I'm out of here. But don't worry—I won't tell Wheeler your little secret. *I* have higher standards than that."

Pushing past him, she left the bedroom, slamming the door shut behind her. John sank onto

the bed with a sigh. He'd done what he needed to do. Olivia would be safe away from laMalediction and that was all that mattered.

Then why did he feel like such a heel?

Chapter Thirteen

The sound of the front door opening woke Olivia and she bolted upright on the couch just in time to see John slip out. She started to call out, remind him that a madman with a gun was on the loose somewhere out there, but she figured he probably hadn't forgotten and being a trained law enforcement officer, probably didn't want her advice. Although her watch indicated it was a little after seven o'clock, the cottage was gray and dim and Olivia could hear the storm still raging outside.

The power had gone out right after she'd settled in on the couch, and based on the sounds of the storm she had little hope that it was back on now. She rose from the couch and took a peek out the living room window. Rain poured from the sky and lightning flashed almost in sync with the rumbling thunder, letting her know the storm was right on top of them. She flipped

the light switch to the living room, but nothing happened.

Great.

She shuffled into the kitchen and put a pot of coffee to brew on the camping burner, then stared out the picture window as John entered the main house. Probably off looking for his missing sister and hoping she wasn't going to blow the whistle to Wheeler about his little undercover charade. Her jaw involuntarily flexed as she thought about his revelation the night before.

She'd accused him of using her and he hadn't denied it. Now that she'd had the night to cool down a bit, she realized that wasn't necessarily true. John had recommended she leave at the beginning of all the madness. Sure, he'd taken advantage of her knowledge and the intruder's focus on her to try and gain insight into the house and into the man who may have taken his sister, but she was the one who'd insisted on staying so why shouldn't he benefit from what she knew?

She poured a cup of coffee and let out a sigh. As much as she'd like to be angry at him for lying about who he really was and why he was at laMalediction, she couldn't blame him for it, either. No matter the heat between them, she was

still essentially a stranger and John was breaking a lot of rules and a couple of laws with his undercover mission.

He shouldn't have made love to her without telling her the truth. That was the part she found hardest to get past. She'd thought there was something between them more than just the heat of the moment, but apparently it was all one-sided. Anyone who could have sex with someone, hiding such important things from them, couldn't possibly care about anything but their own agenda.

Not that it mattered anyway, since a man didn't fit into her life…any man. Maybe it was her heightened emotions being at laMalediction and the intensity of the dreams that had momentarily weakened her into thinking about a normal life. Thinking that someone could care about her enough to be honest and not abandon her. John had abandoned her before they'd ever got started, and it was a cold pill to swallow. Not that he wasn't invested, because that was certainly his right, but that she'd believed for just a moment that *she* could be.

She stepped up to the picture window in the kitchen and groaned. She'd completely forgotten that the window on her car had been shot out the night before. A foot of water was probably

standing inside. The insurance company was going to be very unhappy, especially as she made it a rule to always purchase the rental company's insurance policy.

Well, foot of water or no, she was still leaving. If she couldn't drive herself, she'd call Sheriff Blanchard to come get her in his four-wheel drive pickup. He'd probably be happy to escort her out of town.

Her laptop was still open at the kitchen table, forgotten from the night before. She jiggled the mouse to wake it up and clicked on her email account. The icon whirled for a moment, then returned an error message. No signal. Shocking. She picked up her cell from the table, but it was faring no better in the storm—zero bars. A tiny trickle of fear ran through her. What if she couldn't leave?

The rental car had gotten stuck on her way to laMalediction in just such a storm, and the road was still muddy when she and John had gone into town yesterday. It was probably a river by now, or a bayou…whatever they called them. And without a way to call for the Sheriff, that was a dead end, too. She closed the laptop and shoved it in her backpack, then tucked the mouse in beside it. Worse case, she'd ask John to take her to Cypriere and she'd call a taxi to take her

to New Orleans. She could always deduct the million dollars or so the taxi would likely charge as a business expense.

No matter what, she wasn't staying at laMalediction one more night.

She made a quick trip through the bedroom and picked up her discarded clothes, trying not to think about the night before...how she'd felt so alive, then so destroyed all in a matter of hours. Wasted emotion, and on what—a fling with a stranger that, at best, was over when she finished her book? So it had ended a little early, and a little abruptly, but the outcome was still the same—she would leave Louisiana. He would not.

Her few belongings stowed in her backpack, she sat on the couch and pulled on her tennis shoes, preparing for the fifty yard dash to the main house. It would take her a couple of hours to pack the rest of her equipment and belongings, then there would be nothing keeping her here.

The front door of the cottage opened and her heart clenched when she saw John walk inside. His expression was troubled, but not like it had been the night before. This was different. "What's wrong?" she asked.

He pulled off his wet jacket and hung it on a hook by the front door, seeming to avoid looking

at her. "There's a tree down just before the main gate. It's completely blocking the exit to the estate."

"But we can move it, right? I mean, you have that chain saw, and I'll help."

John shook his head. "It would take weeks to cut a tree that large, and I don't even have enough gas to last that long, even if I wanted to try. It's not going anywhere without a tractor to pull it out of the way."

Olivia bit her lip. "My cell phone doesn't have a signal."

"Neither does mine." John shuffled his feet a bit and ran one hand through his hair. "Look, I don't know how to tell you this, so I'm just going to come out and say it."

Olivia took in the unhappy, almost pained look on his face, and knew she didn't want to hear whatever excuse he was about to deliver from the night before. It wouldn't change a thing. "You don't have to—"

"That tree was cut. Intentionally. Someone took a chain saw to the base of it so that it would fall right across the front of the gate."

Olivia gasped. Her mind whirled with thoughts, reasons why someone would block the gate, and none of them were good. "Is there a way around it?"

"Not with a vehicle."

"He's trying to trap me here."

John nodded, his expression grim. "It looks that way."

Anger slowly began to overtake fear, and Olivia felt a flush start at her neck and move up her face. "Well, he's got another thing coming if he thinks a tree is going to stop me from leaving."

"You can't drive through the tree and you can't call for backup, so he *has* effectively prevented you from leaving. At least for now."

"I'll walk. I'll take only my laptop, and I should still make it to Cypriere before dark. Surely, a phone works somewhere in that town."

John sighed. "Walk? You really think that the person who locked you in the tunnel and tried to kill me last night is going to let you stroll out of here? You wouldn't stand a chance against him in this swamp and he knows it."

Olivia slumped into a kitchen chair and clutched her face between her hands. This couldn't be happening. Not to her. At this house. First the tunnel and now this—for the second time in her life, Olivia was terrified while fully awake. "What chance do I stand here?" she asked, her voice cracking. "Even if I lock myself in the back bedroom and nail the door shut, he

could set the cottage on fire, or have another tree fall on it. For that matter, the walls are so old and thin that he'd probably have a good chance of taking me out just by randomly firing that gun of his into the cottage."

John stared down at her, the angst on his face clear, but he didn't argue with her words, nor did his expression change even slightly when she uttered them. She wasn't telling him anything he hadn't already thought of. Given his real job, he'd probably thought of at least ten more things that her mind hadn't yet gotten around to.

He kneeled beside her and placed his hand on her knee. "We'll take precautions...make sure both of us are as safe as possible."

"He tried to kill you last night. How can we make things safe if you can't even leave the cottage without the risk of being shot?"

"But I already left the cottage. If he'd wanted to kill me, he would have had a clear shot this morning."

Olivia shook her head. "Then why didn't he?"

"Maybe because we can't leave now."

"But as soon as we can call for help..."

John nodded. "We have to find him before that happens...turn the tables by stalking him."

"Go on the offensive? That's crazy."

"Not as crazy as sitting around waiting for his next move."

Olivia blew out a breath. "But how can we turn the tables on him when we don't know who he is, where he is, or what he wants from me? We're completely in the dark, literally and figuratively."

"Not exactly," John said and stood.

Olivia looked up at him, confused by his reply. He glanced out the picture window at the main house, and a thought flashed through her mind. "The drywall dust—he left tracks?"

John nodded. "Faint, but they lead right into a brick wall."

Olivia smiled. "Sounds promising."

"In this case, yeah."

"Then what are you waiting for?" Olivia hopped up from her chair, her energy beginning to recharge; her hope beginning to rise.

"I was waiting on you. I know how you feel about me, and I don't blame you, but I need your help."

Olivia stared, taken aback at his admission, and then chided herself. He couldn't afford to leave her alone, and he had to find his sister. The only chance of doing that meant uncovering the intruder's secrets, and she was the key to it all. "Of course."

She took her laptop out of her backpack and sat it on the table then slung the backpack over her shoulder. "But this time I'm taking supplies. I'm not about to get caught in another small, dark space without backup."

He pulled her rain jacket from the coatrack and tossed it to her. "I found a sledgehammer in the tool shed yesterday. It's coming with us. I have no trouble dismantling this place stone by stone if I have to."

He pulled on his own jacket and stepped out the front door and into the rain. Olivia zipped up her jacket and followed behind him, unable to keep from thinking that she was chasing the devil straight into hell.

JOHN PLACED THE LANTERN next to a brick wall in the basement, wishing the intruder hadn't stolen Olivia's spotlight. It would have made a big difference in the dim basement, and John had been unable to find anything in the tool shed that compared. The lantern flame cast a dingy yellow shadow onto the walls, giving the space a grim look.

Focusing his attention on the faint steps that led to the wall, he erased the fanciful thoughts from his mind. Grim look. Damn, he was starting to sound like one of those novels Olivia

wrote. Unfortunately, the word really fit the moment. They were trapped, being stalked by an unknown person or persons, his sister had now been missing for six days, and he'd been a damned fool and hurt the one person he'd ever felt anything for besides his mom and sister.

There was nothing to be done about it now. He looked down at the prints in front of the wall, studying them as he would those of any animal he tracked in the woods. Olivia crouched down for a closer look at the prints and ran her hand across the wall directly in front of the last two prints.

"I don't feel anything down here, and nothing sticks out as a possibility for a trigger point," Olivia said.

"I think it's on the top somewhere, maybe even the ceiling," John said.

Olivia rose up from the basement floor. "What makes you think that?"

John pointed at the footprints. "Look at the last prints. The toe is darker than the rest of them. Like he pushed his body weight up on his toes."

Olivia studied the footprints for a moment and nodded. "You're right. That's smart. I wouldn't have thought about it."

Despite the emotional wall between them,

John still relished Olivia's appreciation for his ability. "You pick up a lot tracking. And I've read a lot of books."

Olivia nodded. "All the forensic investigative techniques have really changed things in a good way. I've done a lot of research on forensics for my books. Talked to a lot of cops. But reading or even writing about it doesn't make you capable of practical application. That takes a level of talent."

John reached up and placed his hand on the ceiling above them. "Well, let's see if we can practically find that trigger switch. Otherwise, the only thing I'm applying to that wall is a sledgehammer." He ran his hand across the roof line in front of the brick wall, first directly against it, then moving back from it a bit at a time, testing the entire surface for bumps or indentations.

"We know something else about the intruder now," Olivia said.

"What's that?"

"He's shorter than you."

John paused for a moment, looked over at Olivia and smiled. "You're right. I can lay my hand flat on the ceiling without standing on tiptoe. Assuming the intruder only needs to press

the spot with his finger, he could be three or more inches shorter than me."

Olivia frowned. "Which totally leaves out Tom Breaux, the cook. He's easily as tall as you. Damn, he was our best bet."

John shook his head. "I don't know about that. Tom may very well be doing something illegal that he doesn't want anyone to know about, but he's not more or less a suspect than anyone else. My bet is the old caretaker's not all that tall. He didn't have any tools stored on the top shelf in the tool shed. And then there's our friend the sheriff. He's a few inches shorter than me."

"I should be so lucky. That man really gets under my skin. I hate liars."

A flash of guilt passed through John at her last statement, but then he couldn't really blame her. He hated liars, too, even though he'd deliberately chosen to become one. "I agree, he knows more than he's telling. He didn't look surprised in the least at your story, just annoyed."

"Maybe he's stealing the china, piece by piece."

John's fingers passed over a slight indentation in the ceiling and he paused. "I think I've got something here." He pressed his finger firmly into the indentation and a panel of bricks slid

silently back, revealing a narrow walkway beyond.

Olivia's eyes widened. "Wow. I knew it had to be here, but do you realize what kind of engineering it took to make something as heavy as that wall work so quietly?"

John nodded and picked up the lantern from the shelf next to the opening. "Good engineering and a whole lot of WD-40. Someone's maintained these passages well, and I can't see any ethical reason why."

"What do you see?" Olivia stepped next to him and peered into the tunnel.

"Not much. All I can make out with this light is another solid wall ahead, so either the passage turns off somewhere that we can't see from the opening or there's another hidden door." He looked over at Olivia. "Are you sure you're ready for this?"

Olivia stared into the dim passageway and bit her lower lip. "We don't have a choice," she said finally. "I mean, I could stay behind but that's not exactly a great option, either."

"No, it's not."

She took a deep breath and blew it out slowly. "You're bringing the sledgehammer, right? I mean, just in case this closes and we can't get it back open."

"Absolutely. And I can do one better." He walked to a corner of the basement and picked up a piece of metal pipe. "This should do," he said and jammed the pipe at the bottom of the opening tight against the sliding panel.

"Unless someone moves the pipe."

"That's what the sledgehammer is for." He placed one hand on Olivia's shoulder. "I'm not leaving your side for a minute. You won't get trapped down here again. I promise."

Olivia nodded, but he could still see the apprehension in her expression. Not that he blamed her. The woman had been through more in the last couple of days than some cops saw in thirty years on the force. He lifted her backpack of supplies from the basement floor and wrapped the strap around the handle of the sledgehammer, then pulled the entire pack over one shoulder.

Olivia handed him the lantern and turned on her own handheld flashlight as he stepped into the passageway. He took a couple of steps, then glanced back to make sure Olivia was all right. Her face was drawn but she didn't look panicked. Lifting the lantern out in front of them, he continued down the narrow passage about twenty feet when it made a ninety-degree turn to the left. "There's a turn."

"That's good," Olivia said. "At least we don't have to figure out another trigger switch."

John nodded but didn't reply. The light from the lantern didn't extend far into the pitch-black tunnel, but from where he stood, he couldn't see an end. Continuing this way might leave them cornered deep in the basement with no alternate way out. He passed the lantern to Olivia and pulled his pistol from the waistband of his jeans. "Just in case," he said and took the lantern back. "You should check your own."

Olivia pulled her pistol from her waistband and checked the clip. "I've checked it at least five times since we left the cottage this morning." She gave John a grim smile. "I'm hoping I don't get to use it—this is awfully close quarters."

"Which is why we have to be very careful."

"Right, careful." She checked the safety on the pistol and stuck it back in her waistband.

John elected to keep his pistol firmly gripped in his shooting hand and started down the passageway counting off his footsteps as he walked so he could get an idea of how long the passage was and where it might be located under the main house. He estimated they'd traveled thirty feet before they hit another wall.

"I am so sick of dead ends," Olivia said as

she peered around him. "Someone had a serious obsession."

"Or was extremely paranoid."

"Well, I can't really say much about that. I think I bought a ticket on the paranoia train a while back."

John shook his head. "It's not paranoia if they're really out to get you."

"Thanks for reminding me that my impending death is not merely the work of my overactive imagination."

John handed Olivia the lantern and began a search on the ceiling with his hands. "Look at it this way—it'll make a great story once it's all over."

"No one would believe it. Fiction has to make sense even though real life often doesn't."

"Hold the lantern up a little higher, if you can," John said and looked over his shoulder at Olivia. "I feel a bump or something where my left hand is, just behind me. Can you make out what it is?"

Olivia raised the lantern up close to the ceiling, then let out a choked cry.

Chapter Fourteen

Before John could ask what was wrong, Olivia grabbed his arm with her free hand and yanked it down from the ceiling. Then she jumped back a foot from where she'd been standing, her eyes wide and still looking up. John looked up and saw black spiders running in all directions across the ceiling.

"It's a nest," Olivia said, her voice shaky. "You had your hand on a nest of spiders. I am officially freaked out."

John checked his hand to make sure he hadn't brought any of the creatures back down to visit. "At the risk of lowering my masculinity status, that was definitely not cool."

"If it makes you feel any better, they're not a poisonous breed."

"And you know that how?"

"Old houses have bugs. I make it a point to learn all the bugs and snakes of a region before I visit, so I can avoid the ones that may kill me."

John stared. Compared to the women he knew, Olivia Markham was a study in preparedness. Hell, he'd bet she even had most of the men he knew beat. "Well, then that does make me feel better."

"I wish I could say the same."

"I think it's safe to say that the trigger switch is not likely buried under a bed of spiders. I'm going to check the walls."

Olivia passed him the lantern. "Take a peek before you touch anything."

"Good idea. The next batch might be poisonous."

"Or a snake, and I gotta tell you, if you find a bed of snakes, I am out of here. I'll take my chances with the intruder."

"Duly noted," John said as he held the lantern up close to the wall on the left of the dead end and scanned for anything else living. "All that's here is some mildew."

He placed his hand in the top corner of the wall and ran it across the surface, then paused when his fingers dipped into the brick. He pressed into the dip and heard Olivia gasp. He turned around and saw Olivia pointing her flashlight into an opening on the opposite wall.

"It's a room," she said, "and it's not empty."

John stuck the lantern into the opening and it

cast a dim glow around the room. It was small, maybe about twelve foot square and bookcases lined every wall from floor to ceiling with books and boxes scattered among them. A long table sat in the center of the room, a pile of books in the center of the table and a single chair pulled up in front of it.

Olivia stepped inside the room and shone her flashlight along the shelves. "Looks like a library," she said, "like the one upstairs in the main house. Well, except for the two inches of dust and lack of windows and light."

John stepped up to one of the bookcases and held the lantern right up to the shelves. "Except it's not all dusty. Look. Some of the books have been dusted recently. They don't have a speck on them."

Olivia stepped over to the table and flashed her light on the stack of books. "It looks like journals." She flipped the first book open, then a couple more. John stepped beside her and placed the lantern on the desk to light up the table's surface.

"Unbelievable," Olivia said. "Some of these are over a hundred years old." She looked up at John. "Why would someone sneak around the house to read a bunch of old diaries? And why hide them in these tunnels?"

"I don't know, but I don't like it." John pulled one of the dusted books from the shelf behind them. "This one is an album, like the one you found upstairs."

He placed the album on the table and flipped through the pictures. The first couple of pages contained photos of laMalediction from years ago and while still under construction, but when he flipped over another page, Olivia gasped.

"It's Marilyn Borque," Olivia said. "Like the picture on my bed, remember?"

John studied the picture for a minute then looked at Olivia. "You really do look like her."

"What do you think this all means?"

"I don't know, but clearly someone has been researching the family and they must think you're connected."

"That's entirely possible, but that still doesn't mean anything to me. So what if I'm a distant relative of people who died a long time ago? I didn't know them or any of my family, for that matter. What difference could I possibly make to someone obsessed with them?"

John reached for one of the journals. "Maybe they think you know something. You do dream about this place. Maybe you were here at some time and the intruder knows it. Maybe he thinks

you're here for a different reason than writing a book."

"Do you really think I could have memories from that young? Even if I did, it would be from the viewpoint of an infant."

John opened the hard cover of the journal and saw strips of paper sticking out the top. "Look at this." He pointed to the strips. "Someone was marking pages. Maybe this will tell us something." He flipped to the first marked page. Olivia leaned over to watch as he read the page out loud.

"February 11, 1862
Franklin got the word today from his father. He wants him to go to war. To uphold their community standing, the family must contribute to the cause and Franklin's brother is too young. Franklin took it as well as expected. His drunken rampage lasted well into the night and I had the marks to show for it. I took refuge with Sissy's cousin the voodoo woman, knowing it was the one place Franklin wouldn't come for me. She cast a spell for me—a spell of protection. I told her that with Franklin gone, I didn't need protection, but she insisted. She said the spirits spoke to her, that they told her I

was in great peril. If it were anyone else but Sissy's cousin saying such things, I would dismiss them as the words of a madwoman, but I know better. I've seen her power. After all, I am her student."

"Oh my God," Olivia said. "Whose diary is this?"

John flipped the front cover open and located initials in the bottom right corner. He pointed them out to Olivia. M.B.

"Marilyn Borque," Olivia said. "It's got to be."

"The woman from the photos."

"Yeah. Is there anything else marked?"

John checked the top of the journal and flipped to the second scrap of paper. "Looks like three different spots. Let's see what this one says."

"February 23, 1862

Franklin left today. I made a big show at the train station because I knew he expected it, but I celebrated with Sissy when I returned home. You can almost feel the burden lifted off this home. The staff would never say anything, as it's not their place, but I can see the relief on their faces. I even convinced

Sissy to drink a glass of champagne. She'd never had a drink before and it made her giggle.

I'll send for him tomorrow. It's been so long that I wonder if he'll come to me again. Six long months of marriage to Franklin have not lessened my longing for him. I can only pray that he feels the same."

"Sounds like no one is sad ol' Franklin has gone off to war," John said.

Olivia nodded. "Since it also sounds like ol' Franklin liked to practice his backhand on his wife and probably the staff, I can't say that I blame them. But an affair? That's risky, especially in that day and time."

"Maybe they're banking on him not coming back."

"But we already know he did. He killed her, remember?"

John frowned. "Maybe we've found the reason why."

"True. He wouldn't be the first husband to kill his wife over another man. What about the last marker?"

John flipped the pages to the last marked entry.

"March 10, 1862

He came to me, my love. It's as if we were never apart. My heart sings with joy at the very sight of him and my body quakes with his every touch. I cannot get enough of him, even though we spend almost all our hours together.

If only I weren't tied to this dreadful house out in the middle of nowhere. I know well why Franklin built here, surrounding me with swamps and bayous. He knew if I were still in New Orleans, I could find a way to be happy, despite being married to him. But here, in this desolate place, an emptiness sometimes overcomes me, even when I am with my beloved.

Sissy's cousin says the house is lonely and it's tugging at my soul to fill it up. I know it's a thing of brick and mortar, but there are times when I'm certain I'm alone and I can still feel something watching. I will ask Sissy's cousin to cast a spell of protection for me. My sleep is troubled with dreams and I wake restless but unable to remember them with any clarity.

I sometimes wonder if I am afraid to remember."

Olivia crossed her arms across her chest and shuddered. "Okay, that's just creepy. She talks about this house like it's alive."

"Not exactly a stretch from a woman practicing voodoo."

"No, I guess it's not. I just…what in the world have I gotten in the middle of?"

"I don't know," he said, "but someone has been doing a lot of studying…a lot of research."

"On what? I'll give you those passages in the journal are fascinating just because of the subject matter, but what do they have to do with me? What purpose do they serve for the intruder? Why *those* particular passages?"

"I don't know, but I think we need to do some reading. There's got to be a link somewhere. Maybe we can find it." John stared down at the journal and frowned. "Why does she say 'Sissy's cousin' but she never gives the woman's name?"

"I can only guess that it's superstition. Writing her given name may give the spirits power over the cousin."

John stared. "Seriously?"

"I don't know for sure, but it wouldn't surprise me. A lot of the old cultures are centered around fear of spirits and being used as portals or gates

for them to cross. I don't know that much about voodoo, so I'm just guessing."

"That makes as much sense as anything else, I guess. I think we should take these back with us to the cottage so we can read them thoroughly."

Olivia nodded. "There was a laundry basket on the washing machine. We could bring it back and load it up, but then he's going to know we were here." She lowered her eyes to the table. "And none of this helps find your sister. I'm…I'm afraid for her. If he finds out we were here."

John blew out a breath, considering her words, but he already knew she was right. If they took the books the intruder would know they'd found the tunnel, but they couldn't exactly set up shop in this room, either. Damn it! Every step forward he took in locating the intruder seemed to be one more barrier to finding his sister, and after the shooting incident John had no doubt that the intruder would kill to get what he wanted.

He looked at Olivia, who was staring at him, probably hoping he'd come up with a solution. As she opened her mouth to speak, John heard an almost inaudible shuffle in the passage. He placed his finger over her lips and nodded toward the doorway. Olivia's eyes widened and her body went rigid.

Easing his pistol out of his waistband, John crept toward the doorway. He motioned to Olivia to duck down behind the table and she slid to the basement floor, the top of her head and her pistol the only things above the table's surface. He was only a couple of feet from the doorway when the door began to slide silently back into place.

He heard Olivia gasp as he dove for the closing wall of bricks, but he wasn't quick enough. The wall slid silently into place, closing them off completely from the passage. John slammed a fist into the wall in frustration, his heartbeat pounding in his ears. Always so close, but not within his grasp.

He ran his hands across the ceiling in front of the doorway, knowing already that it was pointless to hurry. The intruder had a huge advantage on disappearing and John knew he was long gone. Olivia stepped up beside him and silently began to search the wall next to the doorway. A couple of seconds later, she pressed a spot on the wall and the brick wall slid back. John lifted his pistol in ready position and moved quickly around the corner, but the passageway was empty.

He stepped back into the room and shook his head at Olivia. "He's gone."

Olivia glanced at the opening then back at John. "You're sure he was out there? I mean, there could be a delay on the door…"

John shook his head. "He was there. I heard him, just like I heard you that first night. He's good, but he's not a ghost."

"Well, I guess there's one positive thing."

"Really? And what in the world could that be?"

"He knows we found the room, so we can take all the books we want."

John sighed. "I suppose you're right. Do you want to go back and get the laundry basket now?"

"No," Olivia said as she gathered the books on the table and stuffed them in her backpack. "We need to keep looking for your sister. The books on the table are probably the most important ones. We can start with those."

John nodded, relieved that he wasn't going to have to choose between continuing to look for his sister and sticking close to Olivia. "Can you handle the backpack? I don't want to put additional strain on your ankle, but I'd like to be ready for action if needed."

"My ankle's barely sore, and I'd rather you had one hand wrapped around your gun and the other around the intruder's throat."

John lifted the lantern from the table and handed it to Olivia. "That can be arranged."

FIVE HOURS LATER, Olivia laid the backpack on the kitchen table in the caretaker's cottage and sank into the chair in front of it. She buried her head between her arms on the table and tried to choke back the disappointment she felt. Over six hours combing the tunnels in the basement, looking for secret doors and rooms, avoiding spiders and the library room was the only find they'd made.

She heard John open the refrigerator behind her, but she didn't even lift an eyebrow.

"You all right?" he asked.

"Yeah. I'm just too tired to move. I think I'll just sleep right here with my clothes on, okay?"

"You ought to take a hot shower while we still have power. That should make you feel better."

Olivia lifted her head as he slid into the chair across from her and pushed a beer across the table. "A shower would require taking off my shoes and clothes and then there's that ten-step walk from here to the bathroom. I'd have to turn the faucets on and off, and I gotta be quite honest, the thought of towel-drying makes me want to weep."

John smiled. "You writers aren't exactly a hardy bunch, are you?"

"Depends on what you call hardy. If you mean are we normally equipped to deal with stalkers and gunfire and being trapped in remote areas surrounded by numerous creatures that can kill you with no viable means of escape or contact with the outside world, then no, we're not hardy."

He raised one eyebrow. "But no shortage of words, I see."

"The day I have a shortage of words is the day I'm…never mind." The last thing she needed to bring to the forefront of John's mind was death. She grabbed the beer and took a huge drink, wincing at the bitterness.

"More of a wine person?"

"Actually, I'm more of a coffee person. Even late at night. It doesn't keep me awake—the caffeine. I guess I'm just wired differently, but I drink it for the taste. Or on a chilly night, I like to wrap my hands around a warm mug." She looked over at John, then down at the table. "Stupid, right?"

"No. I used to yell at my sister for taking the last cup of coffee. She doesn't even like coffee, but she used to say the same thing—that she liked the feel of the warm mug in her hands.

And the smell. She loves the smell of coffee brewing."

Olivia could hear in John's voice how much he cared about his sister, and she couldn't help but wonder about this man who was such an enigma. "Tell me about her. I mean, if you want to."

"Rachel is beautiful, and smart, and hard-headed, like our mother. She's a grad student working on her master's thesis in architecture. That's why she came to laMalediction. It was on a list of houses she wanted to visit for her thesis." He gave Olivia a sad smile. "She'd like you, especially your knowledge of old homes."

"And your parents. You said she was your half sister—did your parents divorce?"

"No. My dad was a policeman. He was killed on the job when I was five."

A wave of sympathy washed over Olivia. "That's so sad. I sometimes think it's easier for me because I've never known what I was missing since I can't remember my parents. So your mother remarried. Is your stepfather nice? Is he a cop, too?"

"My stepfather was very nice. He was the attorney that handled my dad's will. I think Mom believed if she married a man who wore a suit to work and sat behind a desk, that she wouldn't lose him, but he died four years ago of a heart

attack. We had no warning, and it hit my mom and sister hard."

Olivia felt her heart clench. "I can't imagine… to lose not just one, but two men you loved. She must be remarkable to have held it together."

"She is remarkable, but everyone has their limit, and I'm afraid Rachel may be hers. Mom's in the hospital right now undergoing chemo. She's getting weaker every day, and I worry that if I don't find Rachel alive and soon that she'll give up."

"Oh, John, I am so sorry. How awful that must be for her and you. And you can't even contact her now to reassure her." Olivia bolted up in her seat. "The cell phones!" She reached for her cell phone that used to be attached to her laptop and realized the cord hung on the side of the table, her phone nowhere in sight.

"It's gone." She looked at John, unable to control the waver in her voice. "Please tell me you had your phone in your pocket."

John rushed into the bedroom and Olivia heard him curse. He walked back into the kitchen. "Stupid! I should have thought about the phones."

Olivia shook her head. "You're not stupid. You're just stressed and dealing with a huge unknown. I didn't think about it, either."

"But I should have. Why should we assume he hasn't gone through everything in this cottage?"

"It's pointless to blame yourself now, and with the way the rain is still coming down, we both know they would have been useless, anyway."

"Right now, maybe, but after the storm we could have called for backup. Damn it!" John slammed his hand on the table, causing Olivia's laptop to jump.

Olivia glanced at the useless computer and saw a piece of paper sticking out from the inside of the laptop. She pulled the laptop over to her and lifted the top. A single piece of paper lay inside. Olivia sucked in a breath and John looked down at her.

"What's wrong?"

Olivia pointed to the paper. "That's not mine."

"Open it."

"Should I put on gloves first or something?"

John sighed. "Yeah, probably so. Hold on." He stepped into the bathroom, then returned with tweezers and grabbed a knife from the kitchen drawer. He pulled the note from her laptop onto the table, held one corner down with the knife and pulled the other side open with the tweezers. They both leaned over to read the handwritten message.

The time is now. Fulfill the prophecy and you can all leave.

Olivia's pulse quickened as she read the words, but her mind couldn't make anything of them. What prophecy? "I don't…I don't understand."

"He left the message in your laptop. It must mean something."

Olivia read the message over and over, her mind racing with the limited research information she'd gained on the history of laMalediction and its residents. "No. I swear. There's hardly any information on laMalediction available, and I'd definitely remember if I'd read about a prophecy. I have no idea what that could mean."

"Someone thinks you do."

"I don't care what they think. I ought to know what's in my own mind. Besides, I'd give him anything to leave here alive."

John pointed to the note. "See how he phrases this—'you can *all*'—it makes me think he's referring to more than just me and you."

Olivia looked up at him, barely able to make out his face from the glow of the laptop. "You think he means your sister?"

"Maybe. Or maybe I'm looking for answers where there aren't any."

Olivia studied the words again. "Still, it's an odd way to phrase it if he only meant the two

of us. But if he meant your sister, then he must know you're here looking for her." She sat up straight in her chair. "And that means he knows who you are. How can he know all that?"

"He probably went through our stuff when he took the phones. My badge is in my wallet."

"But all that would tell him is that you were a cop. If he thought you were looking for a missing person, wouldn't he expect you to drive in here with a search warrant, instead of posing as a caretaker?"

John shook his head, his expression grim. "I don't know."

"Do you think the cabin is bugged?" Olivia asked, the thought of the intruder listening to them the night before making her ill.

"At this point, anything's possible, but he'd have to be nearby or have a server to send the signal in order to listen, and with all these storms, I don't think it's possible—at least not often."

"Did you talk to anyone about your sister when it wasn't storming?"

John frowned. "Yeah, I think so. I mean, I talked to my partner on my cell in here, but I can't remember what I said exactly. I've talked to him in the main house, too." John looked out the window at the main house. "I suppose he could

have overheard me. Those tunnels run everywhere and all it would take is a well-positioned vent to hear everything."

Olivia gazed out at laMalediction, and a chill came over her. "It's hard to wrap your mind around…that someone may have been watching me, listening to me…all this time. At times, it was almost like I could feel something, a presence, but I chalked it up to stress and nerves and being in such a remote location."

"Maybe it was intuition. Fear is a powerful emotion, and we spend too much of our lives ignoring the signals. Maybe we'd all be safer if we learned to listen to those feelings."

"Even if I think it's just paranoia?"

"*Especially* if you think it's just paranoia."

Chapter Fifteen

Olivia pulled on a T-shirt and shorts and towel-dried her hair by candlelight. The shower had worked out some of the stiffness she felt from all the activity of the past couple of days and even though she was tired, she was excited about reading the journals. She opened the bathroom door and the smell of freshly-brewed coffee wafted by.

"You have no idea how happy I am that you have a Coleman burner. Even I didn't come prepared to make coffee with no electricity."

John looked up from the kitchen table. "I'd love to take all the credit, but the burner was in the cabinets when I got here. I figured out real quick why Aubrey kept it easily accessible. He probably spent a lot of time cooking on it with all these power outages."

"If Aubrey doesn't turn out to be the intruder, I owe him big." She took a cup down from the cabinet and filled it with the steamy liquid. "You

should catch a shower while the water's still hot. No telling how long we'll be without power."

John placed the journal he was holding on the table and rose. "Yeah, I think I will. I sorted the journals we have by date with the oldest on the top of the stack. I figured they may be easier to decipher in chronological order."

Olivia nodded. "How do you want to approach the research?"

"I don't know. I figured that was your area of expertise, so I'd ask you."

"Were pages marked in any of the other journals?"

"No. That would be far too easy."

Olivia pulled a package of Post-its from her backpack. "I'll start scanning the first journal while you shower. I'll mark anything that might be relevant, especially anything that refers to a prophecy. You can read the marked passages and then we can divvy up the rest of the journals and look for more entries that might give us a clue."

"Sounds good," John said and headed to the bathroom.

Olivia double-checked the dead bolt on the front door and glanced over at the picture window, now completely covered with a blanket from the bedroom. She eased over to the window

and lifted one end of the blanket to peek out at the raging storm. The rain was coming down harder now. Each flash of lightning exposed trees, bent over from the winds. She dropped the blanket back in place and slid into a chair at the table.

Despite the storm raging outside and the sound of the shower running in the cabin, there was a stillness in the air that unnerved her. She took a sip of her coffee hoping to warm herself, but she knew that the chill she felt didn't come from the night air. Whatever was out there, she could feel it, and although she'd joked with John earlier, she knew she wasn't paranoid. Someone out there was watching…waiting…and she didn't have any idea why.

She set down the coffee and pulled a journal off the top of the stack. Time to get some answers.

"July 5, 1861
Father told me today that I would be married in a month. I begged and pleaded, but he ignored my cries. Mother, as usual, deferred to him. In one month, I will become the final payment for a business transaction that gains Father the business he wished to acquire in New Orleans. Father assures

me that Franklin is a gentleman, and I will
have a big house with many servants. I find
it ironic that a war is brewing over slavery,
but the daughters of the wealthy are traded
like cattle and expected to stay quiet."

Anger rose in Olivia and she grit her teeth.
No wonder Marilyn Borque had an affair. She
was sold like a piece of property. What kind of
man bought his wife? Olivia sighed and turned
the page. Probably the same kind of man who
beat his wife.

"July 19, 1861
My wedding day is two weeks away. It will
be a huge event with champagne and ex-
travagant food and happy people partying
long into the night. Except for the bride. I
barely know my husband, but I'm left with
a bad feeling each time we are together.
While his behavior is that of every other
well-bred man, there's something just be-
neath the surface. Something wrong, and
I'm afraid to find out what it is. He's build-
ing a house for us in the middle of the
swamp. Even with a house full of servants,
I know I will be alone. I think that was
always his intention."

Olivia pushed the journal to the side and took a large sip of coffee. Even tucked away in the caretaker's cottage, she felt something closing in on her. Something malevolent. Something that had been here for a long, long time.

Something trying to break free.

JOHN SHUT OFF THE WATER and grabbed the towel hanging over the shower door. He'd been tempted to stand under the hot water until it ran out, but he didn't want Olivia out of his sight any longer than necessary. He'd known that someone had easy access to the house and that they'd been playing with Olivia and doing God knows what else, but he hadn't really considered the possibility that the intruder had been following their every move, listening to every conversation.

More and more it seemed like that was the case. Whoever was behind this had planned well and far in advance, which led him right back around to the huge gaping holes in the "why." Olivia didn't know more than she was telling— he'd bet money on that—but every instinct told him that everything going on at laMalediction centered around her past. Which left them in a serious deficit when it came to motive.

He towel-dried his hair and ran one hand across the three-day growth on his jaw. Since

shaving wasn't anywhere on his priority list, he pulled on his jeans and a T-shirt and tossed the towel in the laundry basket. A long night stretched in front of them, but it had been an even longer day.

He probably would have stubbornly continued searching the tunnels, even though his focus wasn't what he needed it to be, but he could tell Olivia was ready to drop. He actually admired her for making it as long as she did. The stress of dealing with all those closed-in, dark spaces would have been enough to send most claustrophobics straight into a rubber room. He'd been surprised that she was in such good shape emotionally and physically given that her regular day consisted mostly of typing and reading.

At least they had the journals. If the intruder thought them important enough to read, then surely, there was a clue in those books that they could use to their advantage. Maybe something that would unlock a buried secret in Olivia's mind. It wouldn't be the first time an event or object had triggered a forgotten memory.

He looked at the closed bathroom door and blew out a breath, hoping the journals would take the edge off him and Olivia sharing such close quarters. The tension between them had diminished greatly from the night before, but it

was still there. The regret he felt at hurting her needled him every time he looked at her, but it had been necessary.

He wasn't going to deny he had feelings for Olivia, or he'd be lying to himself. But he also knew that despite those feelings, caring for another person the way his mother had cared for both her husbands…the way she cared for his sister, wasn't an option for him. His work was dangerous and that was the way he wanted it to be. To form a relationship with someone would be putting them at daily risk for being a widow, and that was something he couldn't take.

His directives were simple—he needed to catch the intruder and stop him from accomplishing whatever he had in mind for Olivia. He needed to get Olivia away from laMalediction and back into her normal life. He needed to find his sister and return her to their mother. And he needed to forget he'd ever felt anything for Olivia Markham.

He strode into the kitchen, took one look at Olivia, and stopped short. Her expression was a mixture of fear and anger, and he was afraid to ask what she'd found in the journals. "Are you all right?"

Olivia looked up at him, her hands still clutch-

ing her coffee cup. "No. I'm angry and sad and angry."

"You said angry twice."

"That's because I'm really, really angry." She gave him a rundown of what she'd read in the first journal.

John felt his jaw clench when he considered that only for the passage of time, she could have been describing his mother, his sister or Olivia. "I don't blame you. That makes me angry, too."

"But I could be related to these people. Do you realize that?"

"We don't know that for sure. And even if you are, you look like Marilyn, not Franklin."

"Do you realize that the best option here is to descend from a woman who was sold as chattel, had an affair and practiced voodoo?" Olivia shook her head. "What a mess. I mean, when I first saw the house and realized it was the one from my dreams, I thought I might get some of the answers I'd always wanted. Marilyn's diaries make me rethink it on so many levels."

"We don't get to choose our family, but yeah, it's definitely better sometimes not to know everything. Still, all of this certainly explains the voodoo angle. It was probably her last hope."

"What a miserable existence." Olivia blew out

a breath. "I didn't find anything in the first journal about the passages or a prophecy…nothing that seemed relevant now."

John poured himself a cup of coffee and slid into the chair across from Olivia. "Pass me the next one. There's got to be something in these that we can use. He's looking for something."

Olivia passed him the next journal in the stack and took the one underneath for herself. "I hope we find whatever it is before he does."

John's back tightened at her words, not wanting to think about the outcome if the intruder got what he was looking for. He was afraid if that happened, laMalediction's history with occupants would be horrifically consistent.

IT WAS ALMOST MIDNIGHT and two pots of coffee later when Olivia straightened up in her chair. "I think I found something." She pointed to one of the journals John had read earlier. "Find that post about the statue."

John opened the journal and flipped through the entries, looking for the passage Olivia wanted. "Here it is," he said and began to read.

"May 5, 1863
We held our first party since Franklin's return at the house tonight. Franklin was

in all his glory, lording over his less successful cousins and their 'common' wives, as he puts it. I don't even want to think about the money spent on food and drink, but Franklin insisted on the top of the line for everything. He intends on displaying his new purchase for the first time. A statue from the Orient, with a purchase origin that he won't provide the details on. It's a plaster creature that favors a lion, but with two breathtaking emeralds for eyes. Again, I can't even imagine the cost, or how he came by the statue, but my guess is it wasn't legal.

He's been obsessed with the thing ever since it entered the house, hiding it in his sleeping quarters and bolting the doors behind him every night. One night, after I'd performed my wifely duty, I made the mistake of touching it. He beat me with a candlestick and I couldn't walk well for days. Even though I know better than anyone what he's capable of, I've never seen him in such a state. It's like he's gone mad.

If he wasn't already mad before."

Olivia felt her excitement grow as John read the entry. "Listen to this," she said and picked up the journal she'd been reading.

"June 15, 1863
Sissy's cousin can no longer offer me protection from Franklin. He was already slipping into madness before the war. Now that he's returned and seen what I've done, I know my days on this earth are limited. At first opportunity, he will strike. His energy grows greater each day, despite my administering the potions from Sissy's cousin. She says he draws his energy from the statue—that the statue is the key to his madness.

I told Sissy's cousin I would destroy it, but she said the power in the statue could not be destroyed—it must be contained. I will drug Franklin's wine tonight and use the servant's passage to sneak into his room. I will bring Sissy's cousin the statue so she can bind the evil spirits inside."

"What in the world?" John asked.
"It gets better," Olivia said, then flipped a couple of pages and continued reading.

"June 16, 1863
I took the statue to Sissy's cousin tonight. She had a violent reaction to the piece as soon as she saw the eyes. The emeralds, she said, are cursed. She removed the emeralds

from the statue and placed them in a pouch for safekeeping, then performed a spell on the statue to separate it from the evil in the stones. We then broke the statue and crushed the pieces until they were dust. We collected the dust in a jar and will fling it far into the bayou where the spirits that inhabit the water can prevent it from re-surfacing. She will set the stones in metal to bind them and cast the spell two nights from now when the moon is full.

I know this is the only way, but I feel overwhelming guilt for the future I am creating for my ancestors. The stones will not remain bound forever. One day, the emeralds will call on those of my lineage to fulfill the prophecy that I have set in motion.

Even if it costs their life."

"Cursed emeralds, spirits in bayous…" John shook his head. "Do you think she'd gone crazy?"

"I don't know. I mean, she was sold to a wife beater, couldn't be with the man she loved, and was locked away in this place from anyone who might have helped her, but that doesn't mean she was crazy. You have to remember the times. People didn't dismiss the paranormal as easily as

they do today, and from reading these journals it looks like she was under heavy influence from her maid's cousin."

"So you're saying she might have been perfectly sane and still believed the emeralds were cursed."

"Exactly."

John stared at her for a moment, then narrowed his eyes. "*You* don't believe in cursed emeralds, do you?"

Olivia took a deep breath and blew it out slowly, considering all the facets to his question. "On the surface, no, but I do believe there are plenty of things on this earth that can't be explained, so I try to keep an open mind. What I believe isn't relevant anyway. Obviously, the intruder believes it."

"And he thinks you're here to fulfill some prophecy. That's the only thing that makes sense."

"Maybe I am." She placed her elbows on the table and leaned toward John. "Maybe the dreams are the part that can't be explained with science or logic, assuming I'm a descendent of Marilyn Borque."

"You want me to believe that cursed emeralds are sending you nightmares as some sort of calling card? No wonder you write fiction."

"Maybe, or maybe Marilyn Borque's memories are buried somewhere in my genetic code and resurfacing in my conscience. Scientists still don't understand the extent that genetics has over our bodies and minds. It's not as far a stretch as you might imagine."

John raised his eyebrows and leaned back in his chair. "Okay, I'll give you that our understanding of the human body leaves much to be desired, but that's still a huge leap to make."

"But it's the only one that explains everything—my dreams, my resemblance to Marilyn Borque and most importantly, how the intruder knew to prepare for me. Don't you see, if he believed the prophecy would be fulfilled, then he only had to wait for me to come. He didn't have to know who I was beforehand."

John sat upright. "But my sister came before you." He jumped up from his chair and paced the small room. "Man, that psycho probably thought she was the one. What if he killed her when you arrived and he realized he had the wrong woman?"

Olivia looked up at him. "I don't believe he killed her."

"Why wouldn't he?"

"It's too big a risk. Think about it. All these years no one's been to this estate and within a

matter of days, two different women arrive… alone. I may resemble Marilyn Borque, but there's no way he can be certain that I'm the one. I think that's why the message on my computer referred to 'all' of us."

"You think he's holding my sister somewhere, waiting for what? You to find cursed emeralds so the sky can fall or hell can rise?"

"More likely, so he can steal them and make off with the money. Just because he believes in some bizarre voodoo spell doesn't mean he's not still a common criminal."

"Practical. I can appreciate that. So what's he waiting for?"

Olivia frowned. "My guess is a day. There's no reference to a future date in the journals, but he must have something in mind. Something soon for him to take a chance cutting down that tree and stealing our phones. He's got to figure that, risky or not, we're hiking out of here as soon as the storm breaks. I figure if the date was far off, he would have taken me hostage."

"And quite possibly killed me."

"I think that was his plan last night. Think about it. Earlier you convinced me to leave la-Malediction. We had that conversation in the kitchen of the main house. He probably over-heard the entire thing."

"And he thought killing me would be a good way to make you stay?"

"I think he thought killing you would leave one less person to manage if he had to chain me up and force me to cast spells to reveal emeralds, or whatever he thinks I'm supposed to do."

"Were there any more references to the prophecy in the journals?"

"No. And we've finished with what we brought from the library. Quite possibly there's more information in the other books, but it would take a while to go through them all. A lot more time than you want to spend."

John stopped pacing and blew out a breath. "I've failed everyone. My sister. My mother. You."

Olivia rose from her chair and placed one hand on his arm. "You didn't fail anyone. Your sister walked into a bad situation. Your mother knows you're doing everything you can to find her."

"And you?"

"You can't fail me. I'm not your responsibility."

"I hurt you. Intentionally."

"No, you lied intentionally. Yeah, it hurt at first, but I would have done the same thing if I were in your position."

John touched her face with one hand. "I need you to know that I didn't use you. Last night was special. It wasn't business."

Olivia felt her heart clench and she wondered for a split second how different things might have been if they'd met at another time. "It was special for me, too, and I hope it's a memory I get to take with me for a long time to come."

John dropped his hand to his side. "Olivia…I…never mind."

Olivia wanted to know what he was going to say, but she knew better than to ask. John Landry already had two full-time females depending on him, and it was clear to her that he didn't need a third. And Olivia didn't want anyone feeling responsible for her. She'd always called the shots, and including someone else in every aspect of her life wasn't something she was comfortable with. No one was allowed to get that close to her. That way, there was nothing to lose.

She dropped her hand from his arm and looked down at the floor, not certain how to say what she had to say. Finally, she blurted it out. "I'm not going to sit around here waiting for the final hatchet to fall. I'm leaving tomorrow on foot. I'd rather take my chances with the swamp creatures than a crazy man obsessed with cursed emeralds."

"You don't know anything about these swamps," John argued. "You're at a tremendous disadvantage, even if the storm subsides."

"I'm at a tremendous disadvantage here. Leaving is my only chance to get help. The main road back to town is too far, but I figured I can hike up to those cabins we discovered and see if someone has a way to call for help."

"And what if those cabins are occupied by the intruder or his family or friends?"

"It's a risk I have to take." She paused and bit her lower lip. "That risk could be lessened if you went with me."

John's jaw flexed and Olivia could tell that a million thoughts, most of them unpleasant, were running through his mind. "And my sister? You think we should just go off and leave her here with a madman?"

"I'll help you search tomorrow for half a day. After that, I'm leaving whether you come with me or not. We need backup, John. With all your training, you have to know that. This is the Louisiana bayou horror version of Vietnam. We've been ambushed."

"Damn it. You're right. I know you're right, but the choices are all so wrong."

"I don't think he'll hurt her until the time has passed. If we can get help here, we can

dismantle this place if need be. It might be her only chance."

"But you have no idea what date he has in mind."

"I have a guess." She pointed to a calendar on the kitchen wall. "Tomorrow night is a full moon."

Chapter Sixteen

The dream came again, unbidden as always, and Olivia felt her pulse increase as she drifted toward the house in the storm. She swooped down into the bedroom, but rather than seeing Marilyn Borque asleep on the bed, she was already dead, her eyes wide open in fright and staring blankly at the ceiling. Blood stained her pale, silk nightgown and spilled onto the stark white sheets.

Franklin stood above her, smiling at his work. He gently brushed a lock of her hair back from her face, then stepped away from the bed and left the room. As he walked down the hallway to the stairs, a door across the hall from the master bedroom opened just a crack. The young Creole woman waited until Franklin was downstairs before pushing the door open and rushing across the hall into the master bedroom.

She hurried to the bed and cried out when she saw what Franklin had done. "Mistress!"

She gathered Marilyn's body in her arms and hugged it close to her, crying and repeating over and over "my friend, my lady." When Franklin's voice sounded from the courtyard, her body went rigid and she rose to look out the window.

He stood in the courtyard, in the midst of the storm yelling up at the night, "I want what is mine!" The Creole woman's face flushed with rage and she pulled open the nightstand drawer. She drew a black candle and scissors from the drawer, then lit the candle with the lantern and placed it in the holder on the nightstand. She cut a lock from Marilyn's hair and held it in her hand above the candle.

She stared out at Franklin Borque, her eyes full of hatred, and started chanting. Her voice grew louder with each passage of thunder and she opened her hand to allow the strands of hair to fall over the flame of the candle. Olivia struggled to make out what the woman said, but it was lost in the roar of the storm and Franklin's continued cries. Finally, the last strand of hair wafted from her hand and drifted down onto the flame as if in slow motion.

"He took what was mine," the woman cried out. "Give him what he is due!"

As soon as the words left her mouth, a single bolt of lightning flashed down from the sky and

struck Franklin Borque directly in the heart, sending him crumpling to the ground.

Olivia sat up straight in bed, her eyes wide open. She sucked in a huge breath of air, swaying as a wave of dizziness ran through her. A knock sounded on the bedroom door and she jumped. A second later, John peeked inside. She must have looked distressed because he took one glance at her then pushed immediately inside.

"What's wrong?" he asked. "Another dream?"

"Yeah," she said and recounted the dream to him with every detail. "The Creole woman must have been Sissy."

"She could have been anyone."

"She called Marilyn 'mistress' and clearly she was attached to her. Only Marilyn's personal servant would have a room in the main house on the same level as the owners."

John sat down on the edge of the bed. "Olivia, you're assuming that what you dreamed is real. After everything we read last night, why won't you believe that your mind could have fabricated such a story? You're able to write stories interesting enough to publish when you're conscious. Don't you think your unconscious mind has the same level of creativity?"

Olivia shook her head. "It was real. I don't

care how crazy it makes me sound. I believe the dreams."

John sighed. "Even if it's true, what good does it do us? The dream doesn't tell us anything useful. We need to find my sister or those emeralds, as I suppose the intruder would be quite happy to work out a trade."

"But we don't even know that the emeralds are at laMalediction. Sissy's cousin wove the spell in her home. There's never been any indication that the stones were hidden here."

"There's no indication in what we read," John pointed out. "But that library was full of books, and any one of them might refer to the return of the emeralds to laMalediction. The intruder must have had some reason to believe they're here, otherwise he wouldn't be doing this at all."

"That's true, but if the intruder's certain they're at laMalediction, and he hasn't found them yet, then they're not somewhere obvious."

"Of course not. Look at how elaborate that tunneling system is. Those people did not do things in halves. It seems they went out of the way to hide and cloister and secret away most everything. We could look for a decade and might never find those stones."

Olivia glanced over at the bedroom window,

but with the thick drapes drawn, she couldn't tell if the sun was up. "What time is it?"

"Almost seven. I want to get an early start."

"And if we don't find anything?"

John's jaw flexed. "If we don't find anything by noon, we'll leave."

JOHN PULLED a folded sheet of paper out of his pocket and placed it flat on the table in the underground library. He'd spent at least an hour the night before diagramming everything he could remember of the passages, making a concentrated effort to get the dimensions as close as he could to actuality.

"The black lines represent the sections of passages we covered yesterday," he explained to Olivia. "The red lines are where I think the house's ground-level structure doesn't jive with the underground structure. Now, certainly they don't have to. The basement area may not be as large as the house."

"Or it may be larger than the house, but that's not likely," Olivia said, studying the drawing. "At least the drawing gives us a good place to start looking again. This was smart, John."

John felt a small swell of pride at her approval, but knew he had much more to accomplish that day than a paper drawing. He pointed to a square

section on the paper. "This is the library where we are now. By my estimates, it's beneath the center of the house, so passages or walls could extend beyond three walls, leaving out the one that the entry passage extends in front of."

Olivia nodded. "You're right. We followed all the passages yesterday, but never tried to locate another passageway in the library. If this room is central, it may be surrounded by other avenues of escape or storage."

"I'm hoping not, but yeah, this could just be one small rest area in a much larger maze."

Olivia scanned the room then looked back at John. "You know, I've always wanted to see one of those bookcase secret doors. Under different circumstances, I might be enjoying this."

"Under different circumstances, I might appreciate the creativity of the designer of this mess, but as it is, I'm mostly cursing him." He studied the set of bookshelves along one wall. "All the shelves have crown molding across the top that connects with the ceiling. If one of the bookcases moves, there would have to be a break somewhere in the molding, right?"

He walked the perimeter of the room, holding the lantern up to the top of the bookcases, checking every square inch of crown molding for a connection, but the only place it appeared to

separate was at the corners. "Maybe I'm wrong." He looked over at Olivia, who'd pulled a chair over to one set of bookcases and was standing on top of it, studying the crown molding.

"Not exactly."

"What do you mean, not exactly? There's no break in the molding."

"But it doesn't have to. What if it's connected to all of the bookcases except for the one that moves?"

"Smart. You moonlight doing construction?"

Olivia blushed. "No. I saw it once in a movie, actually. But it makes sense. I mean from an I-have-secret-tunnels sort of perspective."

John held the lantern up to the top of the bookcase where Olivia stood and inspected the bottom of the molding that sat flush with the bookcase. "The only problem with that theory is if our carpenter is excellent, then it will be almost impossible to detect the piece that's not attached to the bookcase itself."

He scanned the room again, trying to think of a faster way to accomplish their task. The stacks of books lining almost every shelf made it seem like even more of a task, until he remembered. "Look for places that aren't dusty. The trigger would have to be on the shelf itself, right? If he moved books to get to it, or touched it on a

regular basis, there should be signs that the dust was disturbed."

"I'll start on this wall," Olivia said and jumped down from the chair.

John nodded and moved to the far wall. The first two bookcases appeared completely undisturbed, but on the third there were fine lines in the dust in front of one book. Like the book had been drawn back from its spot on the shelf. He pulled the book out from the shelf and felt the wall behind it. "I think I found something," he said as his fingers ran across an indentation in the bookcase.

Olivia abandoned her search and came to stand behind him. "Go for it."

He pressed the spot and the entire bookcase slid back from the wall. "Jackpot."

There was an opening on one side of the gap and a solid wall on the other. The opening was narrow, maybe two feet wide, and John glanced over at Olivia. "It looks pretty tight. Maybe you should stay here."

Olivia looked at the opening and frowned. "No. I'd rather be trapped in there with you than kidnapped and trapped in a room alone."

"Okay." John stuck the lantern into the opening and took one step inside. "I can only see about five feet in front of us, but there's not an

end yet." He inched several feet down the narrow passage, then glanced back to check on Olivia. She was only inches from him and her face was drawn, but her breathing seemed normal.

He continued another couple of feet. "I think I see an end," he said and continued to push forward until he came to a dead end. Holding the lantern up to the wall in front of him, he scanned the surface for any of those poisonous kind of creatures Olivia had warned him about, then placed his hand on the wall and began to search for a way to open it.

Olivia placed one hand on his arm and whispered, "Did you hear that?"

He stopped his search and glanced back at her. "Hear what?"

"I thought I heard voices."

He went still and listened, but only the faint sound of Olivia's breathing reached his ears. He was just about to chalk it up to stress and her imagination when he heard a noise, faint and muffled, but it could be human. He turned his head slowly in each direction, trying to determine the direction of the sound.

"I think it's coming from there," Olivia said and pointed to the wall in front of him.

He pressed the side of his head against the wall, hoping to hear better and the noise grew a

little louder. It was someone screaming—some-one female. His pulse began to race, and he ran his hands over the wall, searching for the way to open it. Olivia stretched her arm around his side and searched the side wall of the tunnel.

"Got it," she cried and the wall in front of him began to slide back.

He passed her the lantern with one hand and pulled his pistol from his waistband with the other, then stepped through the opening, Olivia right behind him. The light from the lantern spread through the tiny room, illuminating his sister and an old man tied to chairs in the center of the room.

Rachel stopped screaming the instant they stepped into the room and closed her eyes, prob-ably because of the light. "Rachel," John said and rushed over to her, overwhelming relief passing over him at seeing his sister alive.

"John? Oh, my God, John, is that you?" She opened her eyes, blinking rapidly, then started crying. "I can't believe you found me."

John crouched down next to her and directed Olivia to check out the man tied to the next chair, who appeared to be unconscious. "Are you hurt?" He scanned her for injuries, but couldn't see anything obvious.

"No," Rachel replied. "I'm cold and hungry and scared to death, but he didn't hurt us."

A second wave of relief flooded through John and he placed his hands on his sister's cheeks and kissed her forehead. "Thank God."

His sister looked over at the man in the other chair. "I'm worried about Aubrey, though. He's been out for a while. I've been calling to him, but I haven't been able to wake him up."

John looked over at Olivia, who had her fingers on the man's neck. "Thank God, he's got a pulse," Olivia said, "but he needs medical care. He's probably dehydrated and who knows what else."

John moved behind Rachel's chair and tugged at the ropes that bound her wrists, and indicated that Olivia should do the same. "He must be the caretaker."

"That's what he told me," Rachel said.

"Who put you here? Did you see him?"

"I saw him when he caught me in the house, but he's always worn a mask since then."

John glanced over at Olivia who frowned, understanding the implication. "That means the man is someone Aubrey would recognize." John pulled the last knot out of the rope and removed it from Rachel's wrists.

"He's crazy, I know that." Rachel pulled her

arms in front of her and rubbed her wrists, then rose slowly, her legs still a bit shaky. "He put a gun to my head and told me to tell him where the emeralds are. I couldn't convince him that I had no idea what he was talking about. So he said he was going to keep me locked in here until I talked."

Olivia pulled the ropes from Aubrey's wrists and looked over at John. "We were right. He's after the emeralds."

"You were right," John pointed out.

Aubrey stirred and Olivia moved around to the front of the chair to check on him. "Aubrey, can you hear me?"

"The prophecy," Aubrey said. He opened his eyes a bit and squinted at Olivia. "Marilyn? It's true. You returned for the jewels."

"I'm not Marilyn, but I'm here to help. Do you know who tied you up?"

Aubrey nodded. "He thought if he wore a mask I wouldn't know, but I've always known. Knew who he was the first time I saw him. Knew he'd be after the jewels. It was written, you know?"

John heard Olivia suck in a breath and he stared at Aubrey, waiting for an answer. Waiting for any reason to make sense out of this mess.

"It's that attorney," Aubrey said.

Olivia's eyes widened and she stared at Aubrey.

"Wheeler? Ross Wheeler is the one responsible for all this?"

"Wheeler may be what he calls himself, but I know what he is. He's the devil spawn of Franklin Borque is what he is. Been trying for years to get control of this property, but he can't until those emeralds is found. I've been here a long time. My people were here many years before me."

Olivia stared at him. "Aubrey, were you related to Sissy?"

Aubrey nodded. "She was my great-grandmother. I got her journals. Know all about the evil man that built this house."

"I think we better get out of here," John said. If Wheeler returned, they were in a bad position trying to move two weak people, one of them considerably old, through the tunnels.

"Can you walk?" Olivia asked Aubrey. She placed one hand under his arm to help lift and steady him. It took a bit to get him upright, and he was still shaky, but maybe he had enough in him to get out of the passages. If they could make it to the basement, John would gladly carry the man all the way to Cypriere if necessary.

"Ready?" he asked.

"Damn straight," Aubrey said. "Let's get the hell out of here before that evil comes back. He

won't let us out of here alive…not without them emeralds."

The old man hurried into the passage at a faster clip than John would have thought possible. John motioned to Olivia to follow. She pulled her pistol from her waistband and slipped into the tunnel behind Aubrey. Rachel followed Olivia and John entered the passage behind them, his mind whirling with all the possible outcomes and mentally trying to prepare a counterattack for the bad ones.

They made it down the passage to the narrow entry into the library. Aubrey passed through the bookcase opening with Olivia close behind, then Olivia screamed and John's blood ran cold. He squeezed by Rachel, who'd frozen in place in the tunnel, and he burst through the narrow opening into the library.

Wheeler stood at the other end of the room, clutching Olivia's arm with one hand and holding a gun to her head with the other. Aubrey was crumpled in the corner, no sign of life coming from him. "Put your gun on the table and slide it over to me," Wheeler said.

John hesitated, calculating his odds. He was a crack shot, but Wheeler had Olivia positioned in front of his body. Even if the shot hit its mark, Wheeler could still squeeze the trigger before

dropping, and if John was off, even a half an inch…it was too risky. He grit his teeth and placed his pistol on the table.

"Slide it this way," Wheeler repeated.

John pushed the pistol across the table and it stopped a few feet in front of Wheeler. The attorney pushed Olivia toward the table. Olivia's eyes flashed from the table to John and he knew she wanted to make a leap for the weapon, but he barely shook his head, warning her not to try. She wasn't trained for such a move and the possibility of it ending badly was high.

Wheeler reached around her and grabbed the gun, then tucked it into the back waistband of his jeans. "I hope you'll excuse me," he said, "but Olivia and I have some unfinished business to attend to."

He smiled and John felt his blood run cold. Olivia was right. He was mad.

John clenched his fists and watched helplessly as Wheeler backed out of the library and into the passageway and then the wall slid silently shut behind him. He yelled for Rachel to come out of the passage and rushed over to the wall. He located the switch but the wall gave one small tremor and held in place.

"Why won't it move?" Rachel asked, her voice cracking with fear.

"He must have jammed something in it on the other side." John reached for the sledgehammer that still stood propped in the corner. "But he forgot to take my backup plan. Check on Aubrey."

He drew the hammer back over his shoulder and swung it as hard as he could into the wall. Brick and mortar splintered and flew in every direction. Before the final piece hit the floor, he drew the hammer back and hit the wall again. The wall crumbled on the third blow.

Rachel was kneeling beside Aubrey with her fingers on his neck. "He's got a pulse and he's breathing, but it's shallow."

"He needs a doctor. He's too weak. We're going to have to leave him here for now. There's no other way." He stepped into the passage and motioned for Rachel to follow him. When she stepped into the passage, he gripped her shoulders with both hands. "I need you to follow this passage out of here and into the basement. I'll prop the passage door open with something so you won't have to find the switch. Take the basement stairs up to the kitchen and leave the house by the back door, then run as fast as you can to the iron gate. That part of the lawn can only be seen from the kitchen windows, so you should

be able to get away without being seen. Get back to Cypriere as fast as you can and get help."

Rachel's eyes widened. "I'm not going to leave you here."

"Yes, you are. You can't help me here and if things go wrong, someone has got to know what happened. Make sure they send a medic of some sort."

He drew his backup pistol from his ankle holster and ran down the passageway as fast as the narrow space allowed. Ross Wheeler had just made a fatal error.

Chapter Seventeen

Wheeler closed the door to the basement and locked it behind them. The butt of his gun pressed into the small of her back, removing any thoughts she may have had about running. Not that it would make a difference. If she couldn't give Wheeler the emeralds, and she couldn't, the end was likely all going to play out the same.

"I can't help you," she said as he pushed her through the sitting room into the front entry.

"You're the one," he said. "I'm sure of it. You're the one who will fulfill the prophecy. I've been waiting for you a long, long time and I've been very patient, but my patience has run out."

He shoved Olivia into the front entry and spun her around to face him. "Now, show me where the emeralds are."

"I swear I don't know," Olivia pleaded. "I'd never even heard of a prophecy or emeralds until

I read those journals last night. Why can't you believe that?"

"I thought the other girl was the one, but then you came. I hid her away, just in case I was wrong, but when I set eyes on you, I knew. You're her descendant, the one who is supposed to break the curse and return the emeralds to their rightful owner."

"And what makes you think that's you?"

Wheeler smiled. "Unlike you, with your pathetic beginnings, I know my family. I am a direct descendant of Franklin Borque and his mistress—the woman who helped him steal the statue. Make no mistake. Those emeralds are rightfully mine."

"If you're the rightful heir, why can't you find them yourself?"

Wheeler frowned. "Because I didn't come from that whore, Marilyn. She's the one who cursed the stones and hid them. Only her descendant can break the curse."

"Marilyn didn't have children. I can't be a descendant of her."

Wheeler's face flushed red. "She had one child…a bastard. You came from him."

His words struck Olivia like a lightning strike. Could Marilyn have had a baby by her lover? If so, what had happened to the child?

"You're lying," Olivia said. "Marilyn Borque didn't have any children. I read her journals and she never mentioned him at all."

"Oh, she had one child—a bastard—conceived when Franklin was off fighting for this country. Fighting for despicable people like Marilyn."

"A bastard...like you?"

Wheeler lifted his hand and slapped Olivia across the face. "My great-grandmother should have been Franklin's wife. If he hadn't been forced to marry that pig, everything would have been different."

Olivia ran her tongue across her lips and tasted blood. "Nothing you say changes anything. I...I still don't know where the emeralds are," Olivia said, her hopes fading as she looked at the madman in front of her. She had no doubt he'd kill her if she didn't produce the stones, and that was something she simply couldn't do.

"If you know so much about me," she continued, "then you already know that I don't know anything about my family. I don't care about the emeralds, and would gladly give them to you, but I don't know where they are."

Wheeler studied her face; his eyes narrowed. After several seconds, his expression turned to one of disbelief. "That can't be. It was written that you would come and the stones would be

revealed to you—the descendant of Marilyn Borque."

"What if there's another descendant? Maybe my being here is a coincidence. Granted, it would be the worst coincidence in the world, but maybe someone else is supposed to fulfill the prophecy."

Wheeler shook his head. "There's no way you coming here was chance. It's you. It has to be you, and you'd better figure it out, quickly. My patience is going, and I don't think I have to tell you what will happen to you and your friends if you don't produce the stones."

Olivia's pulse raced, her heart beating so hard in her head that she could barely think. She had to stall him, convince him she was looking for the stones. Maybe he'd make a mistake. Give her an opportunity to make a run for it as soon as she figured out which way to run. She was at a complete disadvantage in both the house and the surrounding swamp. Her only hope would be making it to those cabins and finding help.

She glanced out the front window at the raging storm, knowing that she had to convince Wheeler that the emeralds were outside. But where? The creative mind that had rewarded her so well in her books seemed to have disappeared, and she was left with nothing plausible.

"You're not going to find anything standing in the entry," Wheeler said. "Let's start in the library. You set up your office in there. Maybe the room was calling to you."

Not the library. Olivia's plans began to fall apart. The library was centrally located in the house. There was no way she could make it down the hall and out the door without him shooting her.

"Now!" Wheeler leveled the gun at her head.

Olivia took a deep breath and walked down the hall toward the library. Maybe she could figure out a way to stall him. She wanted to hope that John could figure a way out of the underground room, but Wheeler had jammed the door behind them. Even if he found another way out, it might take hours to find a way back into the main house.

And hours was something Olivia was certain she didn't have.

JOHN WATCHED out the kitchen window as Rachel ran into the woods toward the gate. The sky was dark and the rain came down so hard that he could barely see her cross the lawn. He prayed she didn't run into problems in the storm or on the road. They were probably going to need

that medical team far more than he'd stressed to her.

He edged along the wall and looked into the sitting room, but there was no sign of Wheeler or Olivia. The faint sound of voices trickled behind him and he eased over to the hallway exit. He stopped just short of the doorway and held his breath, listening for a clue as to where they were.

Wheeler's voice sounded…louder this time and John could hear the anger and frustration in his tone. He felt a tightness in his chest as he thought about Olivia, in the hands of that madman and with no way to give him what he wanted. He'd thought he didn't want the responsibility of another woman, but when faced with losing her forever he knew it was too late. He'd lost his heart to Olivia Markham, and damned if he was going to lose her now.

He peered around the corner and slowly let out his breath when he saw the hallway was clear. Three rooms had entries off the hallway before the hallway reached the entry and four more rooms beyond that. The voices were too faint to be in the first set of rooms, so they must be in one of the rooms past the front entry. The library. That had to be it.

He left the doorway and slipped through the

sitting room into the entry. That got him half-way to the library without having to use the hallway. At the edge of the hallway, he stopped and listened. He'd been right. The voices were louder now and came from the left side of the hallway.

He slipped around the opening into the hall-way and crept toward the library, with no idea of what to do once he got there. Exposing himself was risky without knowing where Wheeler and Olivia stood in the room. If John tried to peek into the library, Wheeler might see him straight off and that would give the attorney an opportunity to grab Olivia. If he jumped straight into the doorway, guns blazing, and Wheeler was already positioned behind Olivia, he could use her as a shield as he did in the underground room.

He drew up short at the library door. Decision time. He took a deep breath and slowly let it out, then gripped his pistol and whirled around the doorway, pistol pointed into the room.

Olivia was in between Wheeler and the door-way, the absolute worst place for her to be, and Wheeler was obviously on edge and ready for action. He reacted immediately to John's en-trance by stepping completely behind Olivia and leveling the gun at her head.

"I would think twice if I were you," Wheeler

said. "Although one has to admire your persistence."

Olivia stood stock-still behind the table, her fear evident. John felt his heart clench and he mentally cursed his inability to catch a break. This was the one situation he'd feared the most. "You can't get away with this," John said.

"Of course I can," Wheeler said. "Do you think this is the first time someone's disappeared from the estate?"

"There have been others?" John asked.

"I had a miscalculation several years ago and thought it was time. A minor problem with counting, really, but one that cost a couple of surveyors their lives."

"You killed the surveyors?" Olivia asked.

"Well, I could hardly let them leave when they didn't produce the emeralds. Besides, a little death every once in a while helps keep people away from this place. It wouldn't do to have many visitors."

"You're insane."

Wheeler smiled. "I'm not insane. I just want what's mine."

John's finger tightened on the trigger. He could make the shot, even over Olivia's shoulder, but it was risky. Even if he hit Wheeler right between the eyes, he could still squeeze off a round, even

involuntarily. With the gun pointed directly at Olivia's head it would take a miracle for him to miss her.

"It seems," Wheeler said, "that I have the upper hand once more. It's a shame you let your personal feelings get the best of you. This would be such an easy choice if you didn't care for her, wouldn't it? Women ruin everything."

He inched a bit closer to Olivia, bringing his gun even closer to her head. "Now, lower your weapon and place it on the table." He laughed. "It's like a repeat of downstairs, really. How sad. In your last moments on earth, you've become a cliché."

John grit his teeth, his hands still clenched on the pistol. He was going to kill them, regardless. If he didn't take the shot now, there wasn't going to be another chance. He looked at Olivia. She stared him directly in the eyes, and he could tell she knew the score. She lowered her head a fraction of an inch then raised it back up.

He said a silent prayer and tightened his finger on the trigger. A huge bolt of lightning struck right outside the library and Olivia glanced outside and gasped.

"It's her," Olivia said and pointed out the window.

Outside the window in the center of the drive

stood a woman in a long, white, flowing dress. Her long black hair whipped around her in the wind as another burst of lightning illuminated her face.

Marilyn Borque.

"No," Wheeler said. "It can't be. You're dead!"

The woman raised one arm and pointed directly at Wheeler. A bolt of lightning ripped through the sky and hit the window in the library, shattering it into a million pieces. Olivia dropped to the ground and John took his shot, hitting Wheeler in the center of the chest.

The attorney stumbled backward and crashed into a bookshelf, bringing a pile of books tumbling down upon him. His eyes were wild and he still stared out the window. "No!" he screamed and put his hands up in front of his face. "You can't take me."

The wind whipped through the window and another blast of lightning lit up the sky. Wheeler screamed and slumped to the floor, his dead eyes still staring out the window. A flash of white passed over him, but John blinked and it was gone.

Olivia bolted from the floor and ran into John's arms. He held her against him, afraid to ever let go. "I thought I'd lost you."

Olivia looked up at him. "Did you see her?"

"I saw something," John said, still not wanting to think about the apparition.

"It was her—Marilyn Borque. I saw her hover over him right before he died. He looked like he was scared to death."

"I think the cause of death was the bullet."

"But she distracted him…made lightning strike the window."

"Olivia, I…I don't know what to say. Maybe it was the storm playing tricks on our eyes. With all the stress and that crazy man ranting about emeralds…"

"I know what I saw, and you saw it, too. We did *not* share a hallucination."

John gave up trying to reason his way out of it and sighed. "I know, it's just…this is hard for me. I never imagined…I still don't know what to think or say."

"I think on the police report, you say that you shot a man who was holding a gun to my head— the same man who kidnapped your sister and the caretaker."

"You don't think I should mention that a ghost showed up and saved the day?"

"Not if you plan on working there much longer."

John smiled and placed his hand on her cheek. "Promise me you'll only stay in bed and break-fasts from now on."

Olivia smiled. "I don't know. Little old ladies fussing over breakfast croissants don't exactly lend themselves to great horror stories."

"Use your imagination," he said and lowered his lips to hers in a gentle kiss.

"Get a room." A familiar voice sounded from the hallway and John spun around to face his partner standing in the doorway, Rachel hovering behind.

"You're late as usual. I've done all the dirty work."

Rachel cried out in relief and rushed into the room to hug Olivia and him at the same time. She was soaking wet from the storm and giant tears rolled down her face. "I thought for sure he'd kill you both before I got help, then Brian's car came down the road and I almost cried."

"I wondered how you got here so fast," John said.

"When I couldn't raise you on the cell, I decided to make a visit. I had a bad feeling about all this. Apparently, I was right. Rachel told me some of it on the way here, but it looks like you two have a story to tell me later."

Sirens sounded in the distance and Rachel ran for the door. "I'm already soaked. I'll go meet them and take them to Aubrey in the basement."

"Oh my God," Olivia gasped. "Is Aubrey all right?"

"Wheeler knocked him out, but he was breathing when we left. I'm sure he'll be fine with some rest and care."

Brian nodded. "I'll go help Rachel." He shot John a knowing grin and headed down the hall.

John turned to Olivia. "I know you don't trust me, and I have some things to make up to you. But if you give me the chance, I'd like to try."

Olivia's eyes filled with tears as the past few days flashed through her mind, completely overwhelming her senses. She'd thought it impossible for her to have a normal relationship…to trust that someone could love her and stay with her, but maybe she'd been wrong. Maybe it was time to take that chance, especially as her heart had already made the leap. She looked up at John and smiled. "What if it takes you the rest of our lives?"

John gathered her in his arms again, knowing that he'd found the place he needed to be. "I hope it does."

One week later

AT THE SOUND OF THE FRONT DOOR, Olivia looked up from her laptop on the kitchen table

and smiled at John as he entered his apartment. He set a cardboard box on the counter and leaned over to kiss her.

"How's the book going?"

"Despite terror week, I'm actually ahead of schedule now. I think my experience inspired me. My editor is thrilled with what I've sent her so far."

"As long as she knows that almost getting killed is not part of your preparation for any other books, she can be thrilled all she wants." He slid into the chair across from her. "I've got some information for you."

Olivia immediately shut her laptop and gave him her full attention. "About laMalediction?"

"Yeah. The cops turned Wheeler's home and office inside out. He had a file with the missing diary pages. He wasn't lying about the baby. It looks like Marilyn Borque had a child while Franklin was at war. Wheeler tracked the lineage from that child down the line until forty years ago, when he lost track of one of the descendants. There's a chance that descendant was your mother."

"Wow. I'm not even sure what I think about that."

"There's more. Apparently, Wheeler's been skimming from all his estate clients. The auditor

has already uncovered two million worth of discrepancies and he expects he'll find more."

"Two million. Surely those emeralds couldn't be worth two million."

John shrugged. "With the historical significance, maybe, but that isn't why Wheeler wanted them so bad."

"So what, then?"

"That nut Franklin Borque tied the entire estate up in those stones. Until the stones are found, the estate can't be sold. The detectives found surveys in Wheeler's office and a family tree with supporting documentation that seems to prove Wheeler was a descendant of Franklin Borque. According to the surveys, the property is full of oil. I believe Wheeler wanted the emeralds so he could claim the property and sell it to an oil company. Then he could settle up the estate accounts he'd stolen from, and sit pretty and rich the rest of his miserable life."

"It's so unbelievable. So what will happen to the estate?"

"The prosecutor has some ideas about that and wanted me to run them by you."

Olivia sat up straight in her chair. "Me?"

"There's a good chance you're heir to the estate. There may be others, but at this point they're not identified."

"I don't see how I can help."

"He thought you might hire someone, courtesy of the estate bankroll, to do some research on the family tree and try to locate the emeralds." John rose from the table and opened the cardboard box on the counter. He pulled out a dusty book and placed it on the table in front of her. "And I have a surprise from Aubrey. His great-grandmother's journals."

Olivia sucked in a breath and lay her hand on the book. "Sissy's journals?"

"Yeah, Aubrey claims that's how he knew about the prophecy and the emeralds. Ought to make for some interesting reading."

"How is Aubrey?"

"Ornery as hell. He said to tell you he doesn't want the journals back. He's leaving for Florida next week and wants to put laMalediction behind him. It will be the first time he's ever left the state."

Olivia smiled. "Good for Aubrey." She picked up the journal and looked up at John. "So I guess I've just got to find someone who's willing to move into a haunted house where several murders were committed, there's almost never any power and cable television and a decent cell phone connection are out of the question. Piece of cake."

John reached down to her and Olivia placed her hand in his. He pulled her gently into his arms and Olivia snuggled into his chest, still unable to believe how happy she was with this man. How content. She turned her face up to his and he lowered his lips to hers with a kiss that for that moment, took all the troubles of the past away.

* * * * *

LARGER-PRINT BOOKS!
GET 2 FREE LARGER-PRINT NOVELS PLUS
2 FREE GIFTS!

Harlequin®

INTRIGUE®

BREATHTAKING ROMANTIC SUSPENSE